Little Lost Girl
Journey of a Soldier

LAKEESHA TUCKER

Little Lost Girl – Journey of a Soldier by Lakeesha Tucker

Published by Lakeesha Tucker, LLC

Copyright © 2013 Lakeesha Tucker

All rights reserved.

ISBN: 1-491-06215-0
ISBN-13: 978-1-491-06215-9

This is a work of fiction. Names, characters, places, and incidents either are the product of the author's imagination or are used fictitiously. Any resemblance to actual persons, living or dead, events, or locales is entirely coincidental.

Sale of this book without a front cover may be unauthorized. If this book is coverless, it may have been reported to the publisher as "unsold or destroyed" and neither the author nor the publisher may have received payment for it.

This book was printed in the United States of America.

To order additional copies of this book, contact:

LaKeesha Tucker, LLC
http://lakeeshatucker.wix.com/littlelostgirl
ltucker003@yahoo.com
(407) 567-8526

DEDICATION

I dedicate this book to God without Him none of this would be possible; and to my sweet Mother, who has gone on to join him.

ACKNOWLEDGMENTS

I would like to send a special thank you to my sister Angie, who is always there to hold my hand. To my Godmother Ms. Jacqueline Wessley, you were truly sent from God. To Theresa Moses, you have always been a positive motivation in my life; silently encouraging me to keep moving forward. To Rob Demesmin, Romeo Gachette and the entire LBS family, I thank you. It was through your guidance that I discovered how to live again; and to never settle for anything less than greatness.

I love you all and I thank you for being in my life.

PROLOGUE: CLUB VISION

There were fine ass brothers everywhere and the club was jumping. Club Vision was the spot to be on a Friday night in the ATL. All eyes were on me and my crew as we ordered a second round of patron at the bar. With our fresh hairdo and new gear, we were looking sexy as hell. Now that's what you call some bad bitches.

"Destiny, do you see ole boy staring at you from across the way?" asked my home girl Tracie.

I slowly looked over to check him out from the corner of my eye. The brother was Tasty! Tall, chocolate, and lean with fresh kicks, a clean cut, and bling everywhere. I must admit dude was fly as hell. With the Patron starting to kick in and the Ying Yang twins banging in my ears; I let a slow, seductive smile creep across my face as we made eye contact.

"Here he comes," said Tracie as she shook her head laughing.

He made his way over to the bar and he shouted to the bartender, "Hey, bring me another round of whatever they're drinking!"

"Oh Lord!" said my other friend Shonda, laughing. "Here goes round number three."

"My name is Lee. What's your name Shawty?" he asked as he got closer to me.

Shawty. I couldn't stand hearing the word Shawty and I especially hated being called that word. I told him my name, Destiny, as I appeared unbothered. I let him kick his game to me for a little bit, then I took his number. The way he kept flashing his money, and letting me know, 'It's whatever,' I knew that this was guaranteed money.

It was time to go and the next spot was on the Southside. My friend Lorie, was waiting for me to pick her up. You know, we were too fly to stay in one club. My friends and I all lived on different sides of towns and came from different walks of life. What we did have in common was that we all loved to have a good time, we were all dime pieces, and we all liked money. We would meet up at different spots, following each other from place to place. By the end of the night, everyone had their own agenda if you know what I mean.

There was one home girl that was part of the crew that missed out on the first Club, Lorie. She was more of my friend than anyone else. Actually, she was more like a sister to me. I was supposed to scoop her up before I even met with my other girls and I felt guilty that I didn't. As we all got into our cars to leave downtown, I told my girls that I'd meet them on the Southside in an hour.

Buzzing on Patron, and rolling on ecstasy, I pushed the petal to the metal as I flew down I-20 to make it to Decatur, then back to hook up with my other girls. Jamming to T.I.'s song, '*What you know about that,*' as it boomed through the speakers; I was feeling really good. Untouchable even!

Then it happened.

All of a sudden, a car comes out of nowhere and changed lanes right in front of me. Now, I had a decision to make; either smash into the car from the back, or go around it on the side that wasn't a real lane. Oh well, I'm going around.

Oh, Shit!

Bang!

My car smashed dead into the wall. It was flipping on the highway. One time. Two times. Can't even count anymore. I could taste the blood in my mouth. Metallic. I saw White Lights and my whole life flashed before me in seconds.

CHAPTER 1

The house was in flames, smoke everywhere.

"Mommy, mommy wake up," screamed my sister Gia and I, as we tried to get our mother out of the house. She jumped up scared as hell. After grabbing her shoes and housecoat, we were all running out of the front door. The neighbors called 911, as we stood outside and watched everything my mother had worked for go up in flames. I was only seven then, when my sister decided to play with matches that Sunday night. The first day of school was the next day, and mommy had just bought all of our new school clothes and supplies. I guess you know that we didn't make it to school that day.

My mother was the type of person that everyone in the neighborhood loved and got along with. She had a best friend named Ann who had a daughter named Shante. She and I were the same age. We went to live with them around the corner, until our mother got back on her feet. I really admired my mother. She was a single parent of two busy little girls and very independent. My sister and I are only 18 months apart, and she took care of us by herself. She always handled her business and made ends meet. Some kind of way, she kept a smile on her face and we never felt anything but love; even through the hard times.

Shante and I became best friends. We went to school together and shared everything. Before long, my mother, sister, and I were moving into our own place again. I hated to leave and cried when it was time to go. I begged my mother if I could stay with Shante, but of course, she said 'no,' and we were on our way to our new home.

We didn't move very far though, and Shante and I still saw each other every day. I would go to her house after school, and we talked on the phone all the time. Things were starting to get normal again. Life was good.

My mom and Ann used to hang out all the time on the weekends. My sister Gia and I would go to the babysitter's house around the corner. We hated those weekends. The woman was extremely large and made us do everything for her. She lived in a huge two-story house that looked like a shack from the outside. We hated the food she made us eat. When we didn't do something that she asked, she would lock us in the bathroom with the lights off. I never could understand how she could sit across the room, spit her tobacco into the fireplace, and never missed. That house really scared us. There were a couple of times when Gia and I ran away from her house, went home, and hid under our own house until our mother came home. Eventually, she stopped sending us over there.

Thank God!

CHAPTER 2

Then came a new boyfriend. His name was Montell. Gia and I weren't feeling this at first. He would come over to the house all the time, sometimes staying the night. Eventually, we let our guards down just a little when we saw how happy he made our mother. Then he started being nice to us. We thought to ourselves, this might not be a bad idea after all. Slowly he moved in and he helped our mother out a lot. This step dad thing wasn't too bad, we thought. He would watch us after school until our mother came home from work. Sometimes she came home early, sometimes she came home late.

A few short months after he officially moved in, life became very dark and ugly for me. On nights when our mother was still at work and my sister and I were sleeping; Montell would wake me up, take me to the room he shared with my mother, and touch me. He made me touch him in places too. The very first time Montell touched me, scared me to death. When I tried to cry out, he gave me such an evil look that I never saw before and have never forgotten.

Montell said to me, "If you ever tell your mom, I will kill both you and her."

I believed him. From that night on, I did everything he told me to do. I didn't say a word.

My childhood had come to an end at the tender age of seven. My peers were no longer my peers and I no longer thought of things with the same mentality. I no longer saw things through the same set of eyes that were once cloaked in childhood innocence. The only person that I shared these experiences and feelings with was Shante.

It was a Friday evening, and my mother had just finished cooking dinner. Gia and I were in the back room playing when the phone started ringing off the hook, endlessly. Our mother rushed to the living room to answer it.

"Hello," she said, while out of breath.

"Girl there's a party on Seventh Avenue tonight, and everyone's gonna be there," squealed Ann excitedly on the other end.

"I don't have anything to wear. Plus I have to check with Montell to see if it's ok, and if he will watch the kids," replied my mother.

"Pull something out the closet, check with him, and give me a call back," said Ann as she got off the phone.

Not even an hour passed by when my mother came into our room telling us that she was going out for a few hours and my heart sank to the floor. I knew what this meant for me. I guess she could sense the change in my spirit because she was staring at me.

"What's wrong baby? I won't be gone that long," she said.

At that moment, I wanted to tell her so bad, but I couldn't build up the courage. I was afraid for her, and afraid for me. I dropped my head and simply said,

"Nothing Momma".

She gave me a kiss on the cheek, and then went to her room to finish getting ready for the night. An hour and half later, she came into the living room and called Ann to let her know that she was ready.

At the age of 26, my mother was a very beautiful, striking woman. She was tall, with a Coca-Cola bottle shape and a caramel brown complexion. Her facial features were soft. She had high cheekbones, and a good grade of hair. Her smile would make your heart melt every time you saw it. I couldn't understand what her man wanted with me, a seven year old child. Ten minutes later, Ann pulled in front of the house blowing the horn. Gia and I were in the front room watching T.V. and Montell was in the bedroom. She went to her bedroom first and said a few words to Montell, then came into the front room to hug and kiss Gia and me, before making her way out the door.

It was about 11:00 pm when Montell came into the living room to tell us it was time to go to bed. Gia turned off the television, and we both made our way into our bedroom. Before getting into bed, we knelt on our knees, held hands and said our prayers. Our mother always insisted that we pray together every night. She said that the prayers of two were stronger than one. After saying our prayers, we climbed into each of our beds for the night.

I said an extra prayer that Gia did not know about. I prayed to God that Montell didn't come into our room to get me that night. I don't know if God didn't hear me, or if I didn't pray strong enough, but a couple of hours later I felt Montell picking me up out of my bed, and taking me into their bedroom. He placed me on the bed and removed my nightgown and panties, as began touching me. He was only wearing boxers. He licked on the studs of a seven year old child's chest, which were my breasts; then he began licking me down below on my private parts. He then told me to lick on his private parts, which was rock hard and standing straight up, stretching outside of his boxers. It was too big for my little mouth and I could not stop gagging. Every time that I accidentally bit him, he would smack me hard on my bottom. I tried very hard not to bite him anymore.

Every minute seemed like an hour. My mouth was growing tired, and I was getting angry. When I could no longer take it, he started making weird noises as he peed this nasty thick substance in to my mouth. Angry and confused, I bit Montell's penis as hard as I could. He yelled out in pain, and I jumped back. He went into the closet and pulled out an extension cord. He beat me so hard that blood was coming out of my whelps. I was screaming, and running around the room naked. Gia had woke up, and was opening the bedroom door. He looked at her like a menacing devil and told her to go back into her room. She was crying looking terrified in the doorway as she stood there, unable to move. He continued to beat me with the extension cord.

No one heard my mother come in. She walked into the bedroom and dropped everything in her hands. If she were white, her face would have turned pale. Her facial expression went from shock to pure anger. She ran to the kitchen, grabbed a knife, and raced back to the bedroom.

When Montell saw the knife he asked, "What are you doing with that woman?"

My mother was swinging the knife in the air trying to get at him.

"That child is rude and disrespectful, and she has a dirty mouth," he said in his defense as he backed up out of my mother's reach.

She was screaming, "I want you out of my house NOW!"

He grabbed his clothes, still trying to plead his case. The knife still in her hand, she swung at him again. This time catching him on his right shoulder. Blood gushed everywhere. He grabbed his shoes and ran out of the front door.

Once he was gone, my mother locked the door. She then wrapped me in a blanket and held me tightly. She was crying, telling me that she was so, so sorry. I cried even harder because she was crying. She still didn't know the extent of what he had done to me. I didn't want to tell her because she was already hurting so much. She went into the bathroom, ran some bathwater and began cleaning my wounds. She stayed home with us the rest of the weekend. No one left the house for anything. Monday she called off from work, and we stayed out of school. On Tuesday we returned to school and our mother went back to work. I saw Shante at school, but didn't tell her about this episode. Life went on, and Montell never returned to our house. My mother didn't hang out with Ann much after that anymore either.

A few months later I saw Shante in the school cafeteria. We hadn't really talked that much lately. She told me that her mother and Montell were dating, and that he had moved into their house. She had that same nervous look in her eyes that I had after Montell had moved into our house. She told me of the things he had done to her and made her do to him. Huge tears were forming in her eyes, tears that she struggled to keep from falling.

"He said that if I told my mom he would kill the both of us," she cried.

I hugged her neck and just held her until she stopped crying. I understood her every emotion, even her fear. Hate could not even begin to describe what I felt for this man.

CHAPTER 3

The school year was came to an end, and our mother was packed our things to stay with our grandmother in Mississippi for the summer. Mostly because she didn't have a baby sitter during the summer months while she worked. This would make the third summer in a row that we went back to our mother's hometown. I think that I needed a break. Too much had happened this year.

All of our cousins and uncles were there in Mississippi, and it was only a two hour drive. Plus, I couldn't wait to see my favorite uncle, Jaime. He would always talk to us and we would play games together. Best of all though, he would always sing to us too. He was crazy, I mean CRAZY about a group called 'New Edition'. He knew every one of their songs and every one of their steps. You would have thought that he was a member of the group. Gia and I always had a ball with him.

After being at our grandmother's for about three weeks, a strange white van pulled in to the driveway. My mother was inside of the van and two police officers; one white and one black. I knew that something was wrong. They walked to my grandmother's front door, and she was already there to greet them. I heard my mother ask for me so I walked from the den into the living room.

The white officer asked my grandmother, "Could we have some privacy please Ma'am?"

"No problem", said my grandmother as she went back into the den.

I didn't understand what was going on. My mother grabbed me and hugged me so tight that I had to catch my breath. Tears were streaming down her face as she looked at me.

"Take a seat please," said the black officer, as he pulled out a pen and notepad. "I would like to ask you a couple of questions Destiny, if that's ok with you?"

"Sure", I said, shrugging my shoulders.

"Do you know a man by the name of Montell?" he asked.

My body froze as if I'd seen a ghost and I slowly whispered "Yes."

"Did he ever touch you in an improper way?"

I looked over at my mom and she was crying, I couldn't help but to start crying too. "Yes", I said.

"Ms. Moore, could you please pack her things, and bring her with us?" the officer asked.

And just like that we were on our way back to Florida. My summer vacation had been cut short. During the ride back, I found out what happened. Apparently, Shante's mom, Ann, came home early from work. When she walked in her room, she saw both Shante and Montell naked in her bed. His fingers were in her private parts, and he was licking on her breasts.

Ann began screaming frantically, "You sick bastard, what the fuck are you doing to my child!"

She tried to strike him, but he slapped her so hard that she hit the floor. He then put his clothes on, and stomped on her while she lay on the floor. He was calling her a stupid bitch while he stomped her over and over again. Shante was terrified. She was screaming and crying; unable to do anything but watch her mother get beat almost to death. When he got tired, Montell walked out of the front door. Barely able to move, Ann crawled to the phone and dialed 9-1-1. The police picked him up about 10 miles away from the house. When the police arrived at Ann's house, she gave them a statement. It was at that time that Shante told them what Montell had done to me too.

The next few days were the most embarrassing days of my life. I was asked question after question in front of total strangers by total strangers. They questioned me in cold rooms with glass windows and white walls. Doctor after doctor was between my legs touching me and looking at me. I was asked to demonstrate what happen with dolls with private parts. I had to demonstrate with the dolls what Montell had done to me. You cannot possibly imagine what that emotionally did to me.

Why ME God? Why me?

After all of the counts of child molestation charges, rape charges, battery charges, and cruelty to children charges brought against Montell, he got 20 years in prison without parole.

By the end of the summer, our mother had relocated us to the other side of town. New friends, new neighborhood, new school, and most of all a new start. Gia had returned from Mississippi by now, and we were just settling into our new home. I liked the new place a lot better and most of all, there were no bad memories. There was a corner store up the street, and an ice cream lady around the corner. I loved going to school every day too. I had a great teacher. Gia liked her teacher as well. Our Mother had a new job making more money working as a CNA in a nursing home. Most importantly, she was home when we got out of school. It was just the three of us and things had started to be normal again. At the end of the year, my sister and I had advanced to the next grade level, and my 10th birthday was quickly approaching.

It was a sunny, Saturday afternoon and Gia and I were on our way to the corner store. We loved to buy candy and soda pops with the allowance that we had earned through the week. There was always this strange man standing in front of the store that was constantly staring at me, every time we went. He never said anything, just stared. I hurried nervously into the store and out of his view. Gia and I bought what we wanted and quickly left. The man was still standing outside; staring. He gave me the creeps. I wondered if he made Gia feel the same way, or was it just me?

My birthday was the following Thursday, but my mother decided to throw my party on the Saturday. I was so excited the entire week at school; I could hardly wait. I invited a few friends from school and also a few from the neighborhood. I was always a people person and made friends easily. The boys from the school had started to notice me too. My body had begun to develop as a young lady at an early age. I was already in a C cup bra, my bottom had begun to fill out, and I had started my period. People were always telling me how pretty I was too. I had my mother's caramel complexion and her good texture of hair. My whole family constantly told me that I looked just like my dad though but that Negro is a whole other story that I will tell you about later.

I had given out all of the invitations my mother bought me and I still invited a few more people. Of course you know that with every child's party, there is a grown up party. My mother called up all of her friends and invited them, and their children over as well. She had so much food available; from chicken wings, to meatballs, miniature sausages, and hotdogs, to crab legs and steak on the grill. Her music collection was out of this world too. Gia and I grew up listening to *Marvin Gaye, Earth wind and Fire, Atlantic Starr, Midnight Star, Teddy Pendergrass, Freddie Jackson, The Leverts, Billy Ocean, Luther Vandross*; I mean the list goes on and on.

CHAPTER 4

School had just let out nervously that Friday afternoon. Gia and I were walking home from the bus stop and when we passed the corner store on our way home, we decided not to stop. There were too many goodies at home. There he was again; the strange man that always stared at me. This time he had this weird, twisted smile on his face. He wore a pair of dirty no name brand sneakers, blue jeans that looked like they needed washing, and a dingy white tee-shirt. His hair was braided, but you could see from the new growth that it had been a while since it was done. His teeth were stained a dull yellow, like he had smoked all of his life. He looked younger than my mother too, but it looked like the hard life he was living took a toll on him. As we walked by, he shifted body position like he was about to follow us. Scared to death, Gia and I started running home. When I looked back, he was still standing there, licking his lips. We didn't stop until we made it in the house. Our mother was already home.

"What's wrong? Is everything ok?" she asked.

We couldn't get it out fast enough. Gia and I started talking at the same time.

"Slow down and tell me what's going on. One at a

time," she said.

We told her about the strange man and how he's always staring at us. I also told my mother how he was licking his lips with a sick look in his eyes. She became so angry. She had the same expression on her face that she had when she stabbed Montell. She put on her shoes, grabbed her keys, and said,

"In the car now, I want ya'll to show me this man!"

We were in the car, and on our way to the store. When we pulled up, he was gone.

"I don't want y'all at this store no more unless you're with me. Do y'all understand?" she asked.

"Yes Ma'am," we both said at the same time.

We drove home in silence. Once there, we did our homework and chores before we started to help our mother prepare some of the food for my party the next day. She was listening to *Freddie Jackson's 'Rock With Me Tonight'* in the record player. This was one of her favorites, and it helped to calm her nerves. We ate, bathed, brushed our teeth, and got ready for bed early that night because we were anxious for the day ahead.

I was rudely awakened by my sister pushing me out of the bed. I got up, ready to push her back, but she was jumping in the bed with a birthday hat on. Our mother was standing in the doorway with a birthday hat on too. They began singing *'Happy Birthday'* to me. I love my sister and mother. That was one of the happiest days of my life. I kissed my sister on the cheek and jumped into my mother's arms. My mother hugged me back and told Gia and me how much she loved the both of us.

"I have something for the two of you," she said as she walked out of our room.

We followed her into the living room, and on the

couch were new outfits laid out with shoes. She bought me a pink Reebok sweat suit, with a white and pink Reebok shirt, Reebok footie's, and a pair of white Reebok Classics shoes. Gia had the same thing, except her suit was baby blue and her shirt was white and baby blue. We had the best mother in the whole world.

After we got dressed, we started helping her set up everything for the party. We blew up some of the balloons and set up the party trays. After everything was done we went with our mother to pick up the cake. We pulled up at the local bakery that had the best cake I'd ever tasted. The cake our mother got was vanilla with white icing and Winnie the Pooh on it. Written on the cake was *"Happy Birthday Destiny"* and there were 10 pink candles on it. I was so excited. Winnie the Pooh was my favorite. I had the blanket set for my bed and a Winnie the Pooh lamp on my nightstand. We went straight back home to finish getting ready for the party.

The guests started arriving later that afternoon, and my mother had the music going. There was a huge inflatable playhouse in the front yard that we all jumped in and we had a lot of board games available to play as well. My friends from school were all there. We played red-light-green-light, Simon says, and hide and seek. The grown-ups had their own thing going on in the back yard. They were all dancing, listening to music, and having drinks. The food was plentiful and after everyone was exhausted, it was time to eat. Once everyone was full, I was able to open up all of my gifts. Everyone bought me gifts. I had lots of toys, and games for our Nintendo. I had outfits for days, and four new pair of tennis shoes; not including the ones that my mother had given me earlier. She had also given me the gold tennis bracelet and matching necklace that I wanted. There were birthday cards everywhere and everyone had pinned money on my shirt. I couldn't have asked for a better day.

The last few guests left late that evening. Gia and I stayed up to help our mother with the cleaning. We then had our baths and were in bed late that night. Our mother went to bed shortly after us as well. Everyone was worn out at the end of the day. Almost as soon as I closed my eyes, I was fast asleep. Maybe that's why no one heard the window pane in our bedroom break before the sun dawned that morning. No one heard the door being closed quietly behind us.

I was taken away from the comfort of my own home in the wee hours of the morning by the stranger from the corner store who was always staring at me. I don't know if it was the cool draft from the late night air, or the swift pace of the stranger that carried me, but I woke up in sheer dread. I was not in my bed. I was outside in the middle of the night, being carried away by a strange man. It was at that moment that I realized who was carrying me.

Oh my God, it's the strange man from the corner store.

I screamed and screamed and screamed; and I fought with all of my might. All of my efforts were in vain. I was no match for the strange man that always stared at me. He covered my mouth with one hand, and held me tightly with the other. He carried me to a nearby high school, not too far from my home. He took me to the back of the school on the football field. I screamed and screamed, but no one heard me. I was being pinned to the ground, on top of the sheets that came from my own bed. He then ripped off my pajamas and panties all in one tug. Holding me down with one hand, he released his erect penis from his pants with the other.

With one swift, sharp thrust, he forced his manhood into my virgin womb and pain instantly pierced through my entire body. No words in any language could describe what I felt. I had screamed so loudly for so long, that I no longer had a voice. At that moment I began to fear for my life. Unsure of my destiny, I fought with all of my might; still, none of my attempts affected him. I hated my self for being so weak. The pain was unbearable. I lay there screaming with no sound coming out, as this stranger continued to violate me, moving in and out of my body.

He was going deeper and deeper.

For the first time that night, I looked up into his eyes. He had a sick, sadistic look in them and a gross twisted smile was smeared across his face. He looked as if he was really enjoying himself. At that very moment, all of my fear had turned into rage. I began struggling and kicking again, but both of my hands were pinned down above my head, and there was nothing that I could do. With hatred burning brightly through the pupils of my eyes, I stared at him. Fire against fire. I spit that same fire directly into his eyes and all over his face. He took his free hand, wiped his face, looked at my salvia, and punched me so hard that he knocked the breath out of me.

I passed out.

Slowly, I regained consciousness. Dazed, I wondered how long had I been there? My eyes flew open in terror. Where was he? Frantically I began looking all around me and he was nowhere in sight. I stood up weakly, grabbed my blood stained Winnie the Pooh sheets, and slowly began walking and sobbing; only there was no sound to be heard.

This was the end of my life as a child.

My eyes had seen too much trauma and I had felt too much pain. Whatever purity of thoughts I had left was gone, forever tarnished. I was no longer a ten year old little girl. My life experiences had produced a certain type of maturity that could not be reversed. From that night on, I vowed that I would never again be the prey, but the predator. No man would ever take anything from me again. I would do all of the taking, at my own leisure, and at my own discretion.

The streets were like a maze as I searched for my way home. The seconds seemed like minutes, and the minutes seemed like hours. I was beginning to think that I would never make it home. Out of desperation, I broke into a sweat and started running. Down the street in the distance, I could see blue lights. I came upon the front of my house and saw my mother standing outside with several police officers. Her eyes were blood shot red and full of worry. Fresh tears were falling down her beautiful face to replace the old ones that had dried. My baby sister was holding onto her, as if she was afraid to let her go. Upon seeing me walking up the street, my mother began screaming my name as she ran to me. I started running towards her too. I couldn't reach her fast enough. She held me in her arms so tight, all of the while repeating "My baby, my baby," as she rocked me. Tears flowed from my eyes like an endless river, unable to stop.

The neighbors had begun to come outside, to see what was going on. After a few minutes, a teary-eyed black female police officer escorted us back into the house.

Once inside, mother noticed the huge red bloodstains in my sheets, which covered my shaking body. She looked at me from head to toe in disbelief. Grass and dirt was in my hair. I only wore the top to my pajamas and the buttons were ripped completely off. My panties and pajama bottoms were in rags, still behind the high school in the football field. I had no shoes on. My eyes were swollen and puffy from the crying. The left side of my face was bruised and swollen from the blow that I received earlier.

A long, deep sorrowful cry emerged from my mother's soul. She just held me, rocking me back and forth. Still unable to speak, all I could do was cry. A few minutes later, the paramedics were there to carry me off to the hospital. After being placed in the back of the ambulance, the last thing I remember was looking up at my mother's sad, smiling face. My sister stood next to her with tears in her eyes.

A few hours before I was on cloud nine. It was the happiest day of my life. Then I felt like it was the end of my whole world. My life was falling to pieces. My brain and body needed some rest and I fell into a long, deep sleep. Hours later, still in a sleepy daze. I began to wake up. When my eyes began to completely focus, I started to panic. My legs were gapped wide open with my heels in the air, strapped in a circular shaped tool attached to the bed. I could feel something cold and hard in between my legs that went inside of me. Then I saw a tall white man with short blondish-brown hair standing in between my legs. My panic turned into fear.

I then heard my mother whisper, "It's ok baby, it's ok."

I looked over to my left and she stood right there,

LAKEESHA TUCKER

rubbing my hair with her hand. I smiled weakly at her, and then began to notice my surroundings. The doctor that examined me had a name tag that read Barden; 'Dr. Barden'. There were also two nurses there as well. I had an oxygen mask on my face, which was connected to a machine standing next to my bed. The tainted sheets were gone and replaced by a hospital gown. One of the nurses walked to my right bedside and removed the mask from my face.

As Dr. Barden removed the metal objects from between my legs, he said, "Hi Destiny."

I tried to say hello back, but no sound came out even though my lips moved.

"I know that you've had a terrible experience, but you are going to be okay," he said.

He looked at my mother and gave her a nod as he walked out of the room.

A police officer came in as he left. It was the same black female officer from the house. Her name tag read Bailey, 'Officer Bailey'. She walked over to my bedside and introduced herself.

"My name is Officer Bailey, and if it's ok with you, I'd like to ask you a couple of questions." she inquired.

I nodded, shaking my head yes.

"Do you know the man that took you away from your home?" she asked.

I nodded my head yes again.

"Where do you know him from?" she asked.

I attempted to speak so I could answer her. "From the corner store," I said, but again, no words came out.

Tears had begun forming in the young officer's eyes.

Then she asked me, "Can you write your answers for me?"

24

I nodded my head yes again and she pulled a pad from her back pants pocket, and a pen from her front shirt pocket. She handed them both to me. As I wrote what I had tried to say earlier, Officer Bailey walked over to the side of my bed, so that she could read my answers.

Next, she asked me "Can you give me a description of him and what he was wearing?"

I described his hideous face, and evil eyes in full detail. I then gave a full description of his complete attire, all the way down to his dirty white sneakers. I wrote down what I thought his height, weight, and build was too. Once I started writing, I couldn't stop. I let her know that he was always at the corner store, and that he would stare at me every time my sister and I went there.

"Did he ever say anything to you," she asked?

"No, he never said a word," I wrote.

"Now I know that this is hard for you, but I need for you to tell me exactly what happened and what he did to you," she said, with eyes full of compassion.

I began to write and relive the entire event, from the time that I became aware that I was no longer in my bed, up until the point when I found my way home. Not leaving out one single detail.

"You are a very strong and brave young lady," she said, reading my last statement.

She looked over at my mother and told her, "If there's anything else that she thinks of, please give me a call."

She reached over my bed and gave me a warm, tender hug before she walked out of the room.

Everyone had left the room, except my mother. She sat next to my bed and held my hand until I drifted off into another deep sleep. After making sure I was asleep, my mother walked out of the room into the hallway.

There she saw Dr. Barden and Officer Bailey talking.

"Ms. Moore," Dr. Barden said, "We just got the test results in from her cultures, the Chlamydia, and gonorrhea came back negative. We are still waiting on her blood work, which tests her for HIV, hepatitis, and syphilis. That will take a couple of weeks," he said. "However, she did test positive for a bacterial infection, which we will treat with antibiotics. She will also be given a pill to eliminate any possible chance of pregnancy."

Officer Bailey then stated, "A sample of the semen taken from your daughter has been sent to the lab to be compared to any possible matches."

"She will need to follow up with a GYN, and you also need to contact child services on Monday morning to schedule further evaluations. The number to call back for her blood test results will be included on her discharge instructions, along with a prescription for the antibiotics. If you ladies will excuse me, I have other patients," said Dr. Barden as he walked over into the next room.

Officer Bailey then handed my mother a business card, and told her to call her if she needed anything before she left.

My mother came back into the room and stood beside my bed. She took both of my hands inside of hers and said a long prayer aloud. She asked the Lord to give us strength for the days ahead and to bless our household. That Sunday evening I was discharged from the hospital, and my mother was given all of the discharge instructions. She had brought some clothes with her for me to wear home. I took a shower in the room and quickly dressed. One of her good friends from her hometown was there to pick us up, her name was Donna. She was a long-time family friend that had been around since I was a little baby. Donna was moving in with us to help our mother out. She had no kids of her own, and she was always nice to us. We rode home in total silence. No one said a word.

My voice was getting stronger, but still barely a whisper. Once at home, mother made me a big cup of hot tea with honey in it. I sat down on the couch, and picked up the remote to the television. Gia sat down next to me. Flipping through the channels, I found 'The Cosby Show.' As I sat there watching their perfect lives, I couldn't help but wonder why my life was filled with so much pain and why couldn't we live like that? There was no answer. Somehow I knew that life would never be normal again, and that this was only the beginning.

The next few days were crazy. Our mother took a weed off from work, and I was out of school for the week. Gia went to school every day though, and Aunt Donna was there to walk her to and from the bus stop. Meanwhile, my mother and I went from appointment, to appointment. It was one therapist after the other.

Man, I hated those dolls. The questions, too many questions. What else did these people want me to say? I had repeated the story over and over again. I wish they would just leave me alone. I had enough. I would no longer answer anymore of their questions. I simply sat there and stared at the blank white wall behind them. I had nothing else to say. These people didn't care about me, and I didn't care about them. The only people who cared were my mother, my sister, and Aunt Donna. No one else.

I returned to school the following week, and my

mother returned to work.   She seemed to be in a type of depression. She didn't smile or talk as much. No one did for that matter. I was glad that Aunt Donna was there. For some reason, she brought a kind of balance to the house. A week later, my blood test results were in. Everything came back negative.

Thank you Lord.

After that, the tension seemed to loosen a little and my mother started smiling a little bit more. Shortly after that, she received a call from Officer Bailey. She was calling to give my mother an update on the case. The corner store had been under constant surveillance. No one knew his name, or where he lived. Helicopters had flown around in search for him. There was nothing that could be found. People recognized him from my description, but no one seemed to know him. It's as if he just disappeared, vanished into thin air. No name, no address, no clues. Lord, please forgive me, but I hope he dies a slow, dreadful, painful death. I wish someone would pin him down, rape him, and rip his manhood away from him. I wish that his pain would be ten times the pain that I felt. Lord, please forgive me again. But that is how I feel.

The weeks passed by, turned into months and then to a year since Aunt Donna had come to stay with us. We were all grateful for her presence. My old bed had become hers.   I refuse to ever sleep in that bed again. My mother's arms had become my haven, as she held me every night while I slept.

CHAPTER 5

The school year seemed to pass by quickly. My sister and I had both advanced to the next grade level. We were both above average students and always made good grades. School was out, and it was time to move again. Move away from the neighborhood, away from the corner store, away from the bad memories. I was glad. I no longer felt safe, or even comfortable walking around the neighborhood. The man from the corner store was still out there, waiting and watching.

Yeah, it was time to move again.

We relocated on the far west side of town this time. I was now twelve years old and going to the 6th grade. Gia was just 1 year behind me, going into the 5th grade. We moved into a three bedroom, one bathroom duplex. Gia and I shared a room; and Aunt Donna and my mother had their own rooms. It was a nice place and seemed to be in a quiet neighborhood. My mother had the same job, but we had to change schools again. Aunt Donna had even started working with her though not as a CNA, but in the nutrition department. Everything was good as it could be. After the 3rd week in our new home, I finally met our next door neighbors.

Residing next to us was a lady named Nancy, and her

two daughters, Sara and Ruby. Sara was seventeen years old, and Ruby was sixteen years old. Nancy and my mom seemed to get along well, you would think that they already knew each other. Sara and I talked a lot, and she taught me a lot of things. Ruby had a boyfriend and was never at home. My sister started hanging out with a friend named Rachel from her class. She lived around the corner from us, and my sister Gia, was over there all the time. My mother and Nancy had started hanging out all the time too. The more they hung out, the more I hung with Sara. She showed me how to cook and would help me with my homework.

Sara also had a wild side. She would let the boys from the neighborhood come over and hang out. It was like a party, the music was always loud, and there was plenty of alcohol. You could even get high off the weed smoke in the air alone. This was every weekend. I was having a blast. This is what I'd been missing.

There was one particular guy that would always talk to me. His name was Drake. He was tall, brown-skinned, and cute. He had a confident swagger about himself that turned me on. He was always dressed fly, with a fresh pair of kicks on every time I saw him. A six-pack grill on the bottom row and gold on both fang teeth at the top. The brother was banging. The more he tried to talk to me, the more I pushed him away. This was a new experience for me. Actually being attracted to someone was crazy to me. I didn't know how to respond. Drake was seventeen years old, and I had told him that I was fifteen.

He started picking me up from home after school, and we would go to the mall and or out to eat. He would open and close the car door each time I would get in or

out too. He knew how to make me feel like a woman.
He had me laced with the newest pair of kicks, and
outfits to match.

"If you are going to be my girl, you gotta stay fly", he
would tell me.

He made sure that my nails were done every week, and
that my hair stayed in micro-braids. He loved braids. He
also knew that my little sister was my pride and joy.
When we shopped for us, we also shopped for her. On
the weekends we would go to the movies, and sometimes
to a party. We had been dating for about two months,
and still no sex. We would kiss, touch, feel, and make
out, but he would never pressure me.

CHAPTER 6

It was a hot, early Saturday afternoon, and my mother had just left together with Nancy. Gia stayed the weekend with Rachel and I was home alone. Just as I was getting out of the shower, the phone rang.

"Hello," I answered.

"Desi, get dressed, I'll be there to pick you up in one hour," he said.

I loved this nigga, just the way his presence commands respect alone turned me on. "Alright, I'll be ready," I said.

With that, I hung up the phone and started getting dressed. After pulling out several different outfits, I decided on my Tommy Girl mini skirt, a Tommy tank top, and a new pair of Reebok Classics. He had just bought me a link tennis bracelet, the matching chain, and a pair of big hoop 14kt gold earrings.

Looking at myself in the mirror, I thought, "My man is gonna like this shit".

I pinned half of my braids up, and left the back down. My skin was flawless, so I didn't need make-up. Just a little lip gloss and I was good to go. I sprayed on a couple of sprays of my Tommy Girl perfume to top it all off. While grabbing my purse to make sure that I had my keys, I heard the car pull up outside. With one last look in the mirror, I was on my way out of the door.

Damn, my man looked good, from head to toe, even the car that he drove was fly. He drove a four door candy blue Cadillac, with 20 inch rims. The ragtop was white, and the interior had blue and white leather seats. You could hear the music a mile away. Stepping out of the car, he wore a fresh pair of white Jordan's, a crisp pair of Giraud jeans, and a white Giraud t-shirt. His bling stood out just as much as his car. He wore a long link chain, with a diamond studded dollar sign charm at the bottom. On one wrist he wore a diamond trimmed Cartier watch and on the other, a thick link bracelet.

As he walked up to me, he gave me a big hug, grabbed my ass, and kissed me hard on the lips. Looking up at him, I slowly placed my arms around his neck and kissed him back. I felt his dick get rock hard.

"Come on Destiny before you make me do something to you right here," he said.

He opened the passenger door and I got in the car. After closing the door behind me, he walked over to the driver side and got in.

"Where're we going," I asked?

"You'll see," he said while rolling his blunt.

We pulled out of the driveway, bumping to *Big Mike's 'I'm Serious.'* This was my baby.

For the first time, I think I'm in love.

We rode around, made a few stops, then pulled up in a long drive way.

"Where are we," I asked?

"This is my mother's house. I want you to meet her."

"Are you crazy, we smell just like weed," I said.

"It's cool. My Momma know I smoke. She smokes

too."

"If she asks, tell her you're sixteen, and let her do all of the talking. You don't have to say much," he said.

With that, we got out of the car and walked into the house.

I was impressed. The house was decked out. There was a plush black leather sofa set in the living room area. A big screen television sat in the corner. African-American designer artwork was on each of the walls. There was a huge throw rug with black and gold colors in it that lay in the middle of the floor. The coffee table was a black mirror top that was trimmed in gold. In the dining area was a large dining table that matched the coffee table with six black leather seating chairs around it. There was also a matching china cabinet to complete the set. This place had class.

"Mom, this is Destiny, Destiny this is my mother Candy," he said, interrupting my thoughts.

"Nice to me you Ma'am," I said, extending my hand to shake hers.

"So you're the young lady that I have heard so much about?" she asked. "What a pretty girl. Please, sit down."

As we sat on the sofa talking, Drake was in the kitchen rolling up another blunt. She was a pleasant lady, but she did talk a little too much. I was glad when Drake walked back into the room. He sat on the other side of his mother and passed her the blunt. We all smoked, laughed, and talked as we watched music videos on BET. She was up dancing and dropping it like it's hot. We all were dancing, cutting up, and having a good time. The time seemed to fly by and after an hour or so, he let his mom know that we had to go. She made sure I had her number, gave me a hug, and told me to call her anytime. She was pretty cool, I thought to myself. He then gave me his keys and told me to go and start the car.

While sitting in the car waiting, I saw him reach in his pocket and hand his mother four crisp one-hundred dollar bills.

Walking back to the car, he yelled out, "I'll call you later Ma."

Pulling out of the driveway, he changed the CD to *E-40's 'In a Major Way.'* Now that was my shit right there. We then made a few stops, so that he could make some more plays. After riding around for a little while, he finally finished handling all of his business.

"What do you want to eat?" he asked.

"You know what I want," I said.

TGIF was my favorite. He was looking at me with those sexy ass eyes, handsome face, and gold grille. Without warning, I reached over, gave him a kiss, and grabbed his dick.

"Damn baby, you sure that you're ready for this?" he asked.

"I was born ready," I replied, still rubbing on his dick.

"Come on Destiny, let's go," he said.

On our way to Friday's we smoked another blunt. I was good and hungry by the time we made it there. I ordered my usual, the sizzling steak and shrimp skillet, and a glass of sweet tea. He ordered the Jack Daniel's steak with baked potatoes. The waitress took our orders and left.

"So what do you think about my mother," he asked?

"She was real cool," I said.

"She likes you, and thinks that you were sweet," he said. "She talks a lot, but she doesn't take to too many people. I don't bring just anybody to mom's crib. You know that I dig you, right?" he asked.

"Yes," I answered.

"Is your mom cool with you hanging out with me all the time?" he asked.

"I don't know, she's never at home lately," I said.

"I saw her and Nancy chillin' at one of my folks house. Nancy is off the chain," he said.

"I don't know nothing about Nancy, but I love my Momma to death," I replied.

"What do you wanna do when we leave here, today is your day," he said, changing the subject.

"I don't know, but I am tired of the movies," I said.

"How about bowling and I could teach you how to shoot pool," he said.

"That sounds cool, but you better not laugh at me," I replied, with a smile on my face.

The waitress returned with our food and asked if we needed anything else.

"Naw, we're good, but thank you," he replied.

After we finished dinner, he asked the waitress for the check. He paid the check, and left her a good tip.

Once we got into the car, he said, "Let's stop by the mall first. Are you staying the night with me," he asked?

Not giving my mother, or anyone else for that matter a thought, I answered yes.

We went to the mall first. He bought himself a new pair of kicks from Foot Locker, a new pack of socks, and three new white t-shirts. After leaving footlocker, we went into Baker's shoe store. I saw the cutest pair of sandals in the window. They were beige and brown with a two inch heel, and straps that came around your ankle, up your legs.

"Those are fly baby. Get those, and we'll find you an outfit to go with it," he said.

While at the register, I bought all of the accessories they had to go with them. A small, sleek purse that matched dead on with the shoes, a pair of gold and cream earrings, and the necklace and bracelet to go with it. The next stop was a boutique called 'Cache'. They had some really nice outfits in there. I picked out a cute pair of Capri jeans with brown trimmings, a beige and brown strapless shirt, and a wide brown belt.

"Thank you baby," I said excitedly as we left the store.

"You know that you're my boo," he said, giving me a kiss on my cheek.

I was blushing from ear to ear. Next, we went into Demo, an urban men and women clothing store. There he bought a button down polo shirt, and a new pair of Giraud jeans. "I want to buy you one more thing before we leave, and I will pick it out this time," he said.

We went into Victoria's Secret and there he picked out a sexy pink satin and lace gown, with the matching robe. Also a pair of pink lace thongs and bra set. I picked up the pink body lotion and body splash.

"Now that's sexy as hell," he said, smiling at me.

He paid for the stuff and we left the mall. We put our bags in the trunk, and headed for the highway on our way to go bowling.

As we pulled into the driveway, we saw that the parking lot was full.

After riding around several times, he said, "I have a better idea, why don't we drive out to the beach and get a suite, that way we would be alone."

"Sounds like a winner to me," I replied.

I really didn't feel like being around a lot of people

right then anyhow. I was high as hell, and enjoying riding around, listening to the music. So we left. Before getting back on the highway, we stopped at a liquor store to get something to drink. He parked the car on the side of the store, and we saw the neighborhood junkie. Turning the music down, he signaled for the junkie to come over to the car.

"What up man?" he asked.

What's up dog," asked the junkie?

They exchanged a few words, and Drake handed the man a fifty dollar bill. Moments later, the man returned carrying a bottle in a brown paper bag. Leaning over the car, he reached inside of the driver's side window, and placed the bag in Drake's lap. They exchanged a few more words, shook hands, and Drake told him to keep the change.

"What's that," I asked?

"Nothing but the best," he said, as he pulled a bottle of Remy Martin V.S.O.P. out of the bag.

He placed the bottle back in the bag, changed the CD to *Crime Boss's 'All in the Game'*, and then we were out.

It didn't take us very long to get to the beach. It was beautiful. There was white sand everywhere, crystal clear blue water, and the skyline was amazing to see at night. All of the hotels and restaurants were lit up. The first hotel we past read 'no vacancy.' We drove past to the next one, AmeriSuites. As we pulled up in front of the office, we could see their sign read 'vacancy.'

He parked the car and said, "I'll be right back."

He walked in to the office and returned a few minutes later with a room key in his hand.

"How the hell did you do that?" I asked

I knew that you have to be at least eighteen to rent a

room.

"Girl, you know that your man got the hook-up everywhere," he said smiling.

Damn, I love his grille. We drove around to the back of the building, and parked in front of the back door entrance. Handing me the liquor and the room key, he grabbed the bags out of the trunk.

"Room 526," he said.

I opened the door and held it so that he could walk through first. From there he led the way. As soon as we got off the elevator, room 526 was on the right.

Walking in the room, I fell in love. It was perfect. A thick comforter was on the bed. There was a separate kitchen area with a stove and refrigerator. There was even a separate living room area, complete with a sofa, loveseat, and television. To top it all off though, was the Jacuzzi in the left corner. We even had a balcony that faced the beach. My man had done all of this just for me.

I looked over at him, and saw him plugging the CD player in the wall.

"Do you want me to fix you a drink?" I asked.

"Would you please baby," he said, while pressing the play button on the CD player.

I walked into the kitchen, rinsed out two glasses, and filled them with ice to fix us something to sip on.

"We don't have anything to chase this with," I said.

"You don't need chaser with Remy Martin ma, it takes away from the quality of the drink," he replied.

"Oh, okay."

I handed him his drink, while he sat on the bed rolling up a blunt.

I sat on the bed next to him, sipping on my drink. Keith Sweat's 'Right and wrong way' was playing, and I was starting to feel a buzz from the alcohol. We smoked and talked. We talked about everything. He told me about how he wanted to save up enough money to buy and open up a carwash. He told me of how the dudes from the neighborhood were all hating on him because he was always getting to the money. He also told me that he didn't want me hanging over Sara's house anymore, and that too many of his enemies come over there.

"I'm going to give you some money to put up," he said. "Every time I give you some money, I want you to save it. Don't spend it! As long as you save your money, you will never be broke," he said. "If you need anything, let me know. Can you do that for me Destiny?" he asked.

I leaned over and kissed him all over his neck.

"Yes, I can baby," I said, answering all of his questions at once.

Gently, he laid me on the bed, and lifted up my shirt.

"I love your big, beautiful breasts. They don't sag, and you don't have any stretch marks on them," he said as he rubbed his fingers across my nipples.

I could feel my pussy starting to get wet. With his tongue, he went from one nipple to the other. This was driving me insane. My body felt nothing like this a long time ago. His lips gently went lower and lower, teasing my belly button. Coming back up, he kissed both of my breasts again. He then gave me a long, passionate kiss. I reach out for his pants, unbuttoned the top button and unzipped his zipper.

"Whoa, whoa! Hold up lil' Momma, let's take a walk on the beach first," he said laughingly.

Embarrassed, I stood up, pulled my shirt down, and looked away.

Walking up to me, he said, "Baby, this is your dick, and I am all yours. I'm not going anywhere, and none of those other hoes can get this," he said. "I just want this to be special for you, and special for me," he said.

"Okay," I replied, in a very shy voice.

The CD had just skipped to the next song. *Keith Sweat's 'Make it Last Forever'* was playing through the speakers.

"Oh shit baby, that's the jam right there," he said excitedly, as he turned the stereo up. "Come on baby, dance with me," he yelled over the music.

"Alright, alright," I said, smiling from ear to ear.

Teasingly, I took my shirt and bra off as we slow danced. I then grabbed him by his shirt and pulled it over his head.

"Damn Destiny, what are you trying to do to me?" he asked.

"Love you," I said, looking at him straight in his eyes.

I began to seductively unbutton my skirt. He eagerly laid me on the bed, and pulled off my skirt. I was now completely nude, with the exception of a thong. He stood up over the bed and just looked at me.

"God, you're beautiful," he said, as he took off his jeans and boxers.

His body was beautiful as well. Damn. There was not an ounce of fat on him. He was 6"1, with a lean, muscular build, and a perfect six pack. To top it all off, the brother always smelled good. Just to think, this was all mines. God blessed him down below too. His dick was rock hard, and standing straight up. I hoped that it fit in my pussy without hurting me.

As if he sensed my thoughts, he said to me, "Baby, I promise that I won't hurt you." Laying in the bed beside me, first he kissed my lips, then my breast. He licked and bit them all at the same time. Then slowly he kissed my navel and I felt the wetness of his tongue as dove lower to lick my pussy.

Oh my God, I was going wild. I was soaking wet and it felt so good. What was he doing to me? My body began to tremble.

"That's right, come on baby," he said.

At that very moment, something inside of me was released. Something that I never knew existed that made my body buck with pleasure. It was my first orgasm, and I wanted more. Drake got up, still laying between my legs, and began rubbing his dick back and forth on my clit. This felt even better than his tongue.

I was going crazy again. "Baby, please put it in," I begged.

"Okay Destiny, but I want you to stop me if it hurts," he said.

Gently, he tried putting the head of his dick inside of me, but it wouldn't go. He started rubbing it back and forth all over again, until I begged for more. With one quick movement, he forced it in, and then completely stopped. I felt one tiny, sharp pain, and it was gone. Feeling my body loosen up again, he slowly began to move inside me. I started meeting his thrusts, forcing him to go faster. Moving in rhythm with the music, our bodies became one. Slowly, we moved in and out, and up and down.

Oh my God, what can be better than this?

"Is this what you wanted," he asked?

"Yes baby, yes," I replied.

"Damn ma, you got some good pussy. Is it all mine?" he asked.

Looking up in his eyes, I answered, "It's all yours baby."

Our bodies started moving faster and faster again.

"I love you Destiny," he said.

"I love you too Drake," I replied.

As my body began to tremble again, his thrust became harder and harder.

"Oh shit Destiny," he yelled.

"Yes baby, yes," I yelled back.

We both came at the same time, with our bodies convulsing in unison. For a moment, he just laid there on top of me and just looked down at me.

"I meant what I said you know," he said.

"Yes, and I meant it too," I replied.

To me, this was my very first time. I had given up my virginity to *Keith Sweat's 'Make it Last Forever.'* I had a man that I was madly in love with, and he was in love with me. I was a woman now. There was no going back, in any kind of way. Getting out of the bed, we both went to the bathroom.

"Can we take a shower together?" I asked.

"We can do anything you want to do," he answered with a smile on his face.

After setting the water temperature, we both stepped into the shower. We then took turns washing each other's body parts. Gently, slowly, I started caressing his dick in my hands. It began to grow, I mean almost instantly. Standing behind me, he turned me around, so that I faced the water. Seconds later, I felt him enter me from behind. With my back tilted slightly, I moved back and forth to meet his thrusts. I felt both pleasure and pain at the same time, as I yelled out his name.

"Where are you going baby," he asked as his thrusts

got faster.

The louder I yelled his name, the harder he went. I don't know who came first, but my body felt like it was exploding. I turned around and he gave me a kiss.

After bathing each other again, we both got out of the shower. He wrapped a towel around his waist and walked out of the bathroom. I brushed my teeth and gargled with some Scope mouthwash that was in the bathroom for us guests. Once I was done, I wrapped a towel around my breasts and walked into the room. Laid out on the bed was my pink lingerie that we'd purchased earlier.

"I want you to put this on; but first come here so that I can put lotion all over your body," he said.

I walked across the room, and lay on the bed as he instructed. He started at my shoulders, then worked his way down, massaging every inch of my body. He moved from the back, all the way to the front. I felt like a queen, and this was my king. When he was done, I slipped into the thongs, gown, and the matching robe.

"Damn Destiny, you look like a million dollars," he said.

I fixed us another drink, while he changed the CD to Guy's 'Piece of my Love.' We talked, smoked another blunt, and drank more cognac. We made love once more on the balcony, and watched the sunset till the wee hours of the morning. Finally, we went back into the room and collapsed in the bed together. He held me tightly in his arms, the same way my mother used to.

Both in a deep sleep, we were rudely awakened by the housekeepers knocking on the door. Drake was the first to hear the knocks.

"Give us a few minutes," he said.

We took a shower and got dressed.

"Damn Desi, you look good," he stated, as he checked me out up and down.

I must say that I looked hot in the new outfit that he had just bought.

"From now on, I want to see you in sandals and heels, instead of tennis shoes," he said. After brushing our teeth, we packed our things and left.

On the way home we stopped at Waffle House for some breakfast to go.

As we pulled up in front of my house, he gave me five hundred dollars and said, "Remember what I told you."

He gave me another long, passionate kiss and told me that he loved me.

"I love you too Drake."

"I will call you later," he said.

With that, I got out of the car and he pulled off.

Walking towards the door, I instantly thought of my mother. Damn, I hope that she wasn't at home. Pulling my keys out of my purse, I nervously unlocked the door and walked in. I walked from room to room, no one was home. I put my bags in my room, and put my money in a safe hiding place. Something told me to go next door. I looked through the house again, just to make sure that no one had seen me, then I knocked on Sara's door. It was early in the afternoon. I knocked at least four times before Ruby finally answered the door.

"Is Sara here?" I asked.

"Yeah, she's in her room," she said, as she opened the screen door for me.

I walked straight to the back of the house, into her room.

"Hey girl, what's up?" she asked when she saw me

45

walking in. "I saw Drake drop you off. What have ya'll been doing?" she asked.

"Girl, whatever. Have you seen my Momma?" I asked

"Her and Nancy haven't been home in almost two days," she replied.

"What?" I asked with a look of disbelief on my face.

"Don't front. You know that her and Nancy are gone on that crack," said Sara.

My whole face went blank. I could not believe what I was hearing. I know that Nancy and Momma was hanging out a lot, but I had no idea that my Momma was on crack. A crack-head. I guess that I had been too wrapped up in my own little world to notice the changes.

Interrupting my thoughts, Sara said, "They have been on that shit for awhile, I'm always finding empty cans with small holes poked on top of them, and black ashes on the top," she said.

I couldn't stop the tears from rushing down my face. My mother is a junkie. Ok Destiny, get yourself together. You are too strong for this. You are a woman now, no time for tears.

"Well, have you seen my sister," I asked.

"Around the corner. Her and Rachel came over yesterday to get some more clothes. She was looking for your Momma too," she said.

"You didn't tell my sister that shit, did you?" I asked about to get pissed off

"No, no, I wouldn't do that, I just thought that you knew since your man sell drugs," she said. "Look at you, all jazzy, where are you going?" she asked.

"Nowhere," I said.

Remembering what Drake had told me about not hanging over there I said, "I gotta go, but I will be back later."

"That nigga must be coming back to pick you up, I heard that he has plenty of hoes," Ruby said, as she came down the hallway.

"Naw, that's some bullshit, that's my baby," I quickly stated walking towards the door.

As soon as I walked into the house, I went straight to the phone. It rung twice before he answered it.

"What's up baby," he said on the other end.

"Nothing, no one's home, and I'm going crazy in this house by myself."

"Baby, I am making plays right now. I'll tell you what, why don't you chill with my moms today, and keep her company. She would love that," he said.

"That's cool, I just need to get away," I answered.

"I'll be there in twenty minutes," he stated.

"I'll be ready," I replied.

No more than fifteen minutes later his candy blue Cadillac was pulling up in our driveway. I grabbed my purse and ran out of the door. He was bumping to UGK's 'Diamonds Up Against That Wood.' As we pulled off, I saw Ruby looking out of their window.

"Drake, can I ask you something?" I asked, turning down the music.

"Yeah Destiny, you know that you can ask me anything."

"Do you know Sara's sister Ruby?" I asked.

"Yeah she's a trick. Half the niggas round here had ran up in that. Why do you ask me that?"

"I'm just asking," I said.

"Have you ever ran up in that?" I then asked.

"Nope, but she has tried to give me some. I don't want nothing that everybody has already had," he said.

"Oh, okay, I was just asking," I said.

"That hoe must have been over there telling you shit," he questioned?

"I am telling you, you better watch out for her, she is shady and trifling, plus that hoe is jealous of you," he replied.

I didn't make anymore comments. I just let his information soak in.

Pulling up in his mother's yard, he said to me, "Baby-girl, I've already chosen, and I chose you. I love you, and I need for you to know that. I don't want or need any of those other hoes. All I need is you Destiny, do you understand that?" he asked.

I nodded my head yes. He kissed me long and slow. It was so passionate that I felt myself getting wet.

"You better go in the house, my mother is waiting for you," he said, breathing heavily.

Before I could get a chance to knock, his mother was opening the door.

"Hi sweetie, how are you today?" she asked. "Come on in."

I walked in and took a seat on the sofa, and she walked into the kitchen. She had the house lit up. I could smell collard greens and fried chicken from the kitchen.

"I just got done cooking, would you like something to eat," she asked?

There was no way that I was turning this good smelling food down.

"Yes Ma'am," I answered.

This food reminded me of my mother's good cooking! Candy was cool, laid back, and had motherly qualities. We talked and chilled for hours. She had a lot of questions. I had lots of questions for her too.

"So where are you from", she asked?

"We're originally from Mississippi, but Momma moved here when I was only two".

"What type of work does your Momma do honey?"

"She works at the hospital as a CNA," I answered.

"Okay, that's good. So how did you meet my son?"

"At a party."

"Tell me, how do you feel about my son? I love him very much, and I don't want him to be hurt, do you understand," she asked?

"Yes Ma'am. I would never do anything to hurt him. I love him too. I really don't know how he feels about me. He got so many chicks always in his face, that I don't know what to think."

"I will tell you this, he cares a lot about you. I have not seen him like this about anybody. That's my only baby, and I gotta make sure everything is right. Do you understand that, she asked?

"Yes Ma'am".

The phone rang.

"Hey baby," she answered.

"Tell Destiny I'm on my way," Drake said.

"Okay, I love you."

"One," he said.

It wasn't ten minutes later, and my baby was pulling up in the driveway. I already had my purse in my hand.

"It was nice seeing you. Make sure you come and visit again," she said.

"Yes Ma'am," I answered as I walked out the door headed to the car.

"You cool," he asked as I got in?

"I'm straight."

Drake was bumping to *MJG & Eightball 'On the*

outside looking in.'

"Can you please turn that down?" I asked.

"What's up baby?"

"I need to ask you something. Did you know that my Momma was smoking crack?"

"Yes."

"Why in the hell didn't you tell me?" I yelled angrily.

"Baby, that wasn't my place. Plus I knew that you would be hurt. I don't wanna see you hurt," he answered.

"Do you be selling her that shit?" I asked.

This nigga just looked at the road straight ahead without saying a word.

"I know you fucking hear me," I yelled.

"Look Destiny, if she doesn't get it from me, she will get it from someone else. Her and Nancy be gone on that shit, and I rather her buy it from me, than that bullshit everybody else be serving. I try to look out for her, and not let nobody fuck with her since you're my lady," he said with an irritated tone.

We were pulling up in front of my house.

"Don't be selling my Momma that shit," I said angrily as I got out of the car.

"Call me later," he yelled as he pulled off.

I so mad I could hardly get my key in the door. The living room was empty, and the T.V. was on. I picked up the remote and turned it off. Momma was in her room, and the door was closed. Slowly, I cracked the door open just to make sure she was there. She was asleep. Aunt Donna was in her room fast asleep as well. Walking in my room, I saw Gia sitting on the bed watching television.

"How long has Momma been back?" I asked.

"Just a little while, she went straight into her room and went to sleep," Gia answered.

"Why are you still up?" I asked.

"I was waiting for you to get home."

"Well, I'm here now, so get some sleep. We have to be up early."

I quickly changed into my pajamas, and turned the television and lights out. Moments later, we were both fast asleep.

CHAPTER 7

The rest of the week flew by for me. It was school for us, and work for my mother and Aunt Donna. It was Friday evening, and Gia and I had just made it home from school when the phone rang.

"Hello," I answered.

"Hey baby," said Drake. "I'm coming to get you. How long will it take for you to get ready," he asked?

I hadn't seen my baby all week long, and I was missing him. No one was home so I was ready to go.

"Give me about an hour to get dressed," I said looking at the clock.

"Be ready."

"Alright," I answered, hardly able to contain my excitement.

"One," he said, before hanging up.

"Where are you going?" Gia asked.

I just shrugged my shoulders, and continued to pack my bag.

"Well, when are you coming home?"

"Probably tomorrow or Sunday. Here's some money for you and Rachel to hang out this weekend," I told her handing her a fifty dollar bill.

"Thank you! I love you," she exclaimed happily and

hugged my neck.

"I love you back."

Drake was pulling up in the driveway, I could hear the bass from his car beating up the block. I grabbed my purse and backpack before I headed out the door. As soon as I got in the car he leaned over and gave me a kiss.

"You look good baby," he said looking me up and down.

"Baby, you always look good," I said.

He turned the music up and handed me a blunt. We were on our way to the beach bumping *UGK's 'Diamonds Up Against that Wood'* all the way there.

He rented a room at the same place as the first time. It was already paid for, and he had the key. When I walked in, I saw a big bottle of Remy Martin already popped, chilled, and sitting in a bucket of ice. Drake walked over to the CD player and put in *Escape's* song *'Understanding.'* Shopping bags were all over the living room area.

As if he were reading my thoughts, he said, "I was at the mall today looking for the new Jordan's so I grabbed something for you too. You know I like for my baby to look good. Go ahead Desi, try it on."

I tried on outfit after outfit, each one completed with all the proper accessories; belt, handbag, earrings, and heels to match.

"Who helped you pick this out? I just know you didn't do this by yourself." I questioned.

"What you trying to say? That your man don't have any style?" he asked with a playful grin on his face. "Come here girl, I've been wanting on you all week long."

He pulled me into his arms and gave me a slow, passionate kiss. Just as my knees were starting to get weak, he laid me on the bed. Before I knew it I was completely naked, breathing heavily, and wanting more. He stood up and just stared at me.

"Baby, I am going to massage every inch of your body," he said.

Drake stripped down to his boxers and walked over to the shopping bags. He returned to the bed carrying fragranced body oil. Gently, he turned me on my stomach and started touching every part of my body. This felt like heaven. He was awakening every sense in me. We explored each other's body, as if it was our very first time. He taught me things about myself that I never knew existed. We made wild, passionate love the entire weekend. No one left the room for anything. Take-out food was ordered and delivered. I was his only queen, and he was my only king. We pleased each to no end. I was in love.

It was Sunday early evening when Drake dropped me back home. He helped me with my bags, and walked me to the door. He kissed me on my cheek, and walked back to his car. I used my keys and walked in the house. Aunt Donna was on the couch, Momma was in her room asleep, and Gia was in our room.

"What's up Auntie," I asked as I walked straight to the back.

"Ooh, you are in trouble. Momma is mad at you," Gia said as soon as she saw me.

"How long has she been sleep," I asked.

"All day, she came home this morning."

I put my pajamas on and climbed into bed. We watched television until the both of us were asleep.

The next morning, we got up and dressed for school. We were on our way out the door when I heard, "Destiny." My mother was calling me from her room. I already knew what this was about.

"Ma'am," I answered as I walked into her room.

"You know what I want? Who the hell do you think you are, that you can stay out like a grown ass woman all weekend long? You don't pay no bills around here, and you are not grown!" she yelled.

I just stood there and silently looked down. I mean, what was I supposed to say, she was right. Don't get me wrong, that was not going to stop me from doing what I wanted to do, but who was I to argue?

"You are 14yrs old, a child, and you are going to start acting like one. Everyday when you come home from school, I want you in your room. Do you understand me?" she asked.

Yeah right. I just smiled. How is she gonna enforce that and she's hardly ever here? She's never at home between work and the streets on the weekends.

"Okay mom, I'll do that if you promise to stop using drugs, and spend more time with me and my sister," I said.

I wasn't trying to be funny or anything, I was serious. I love my Momma to death, and I miss the three of us doing things together. I wanted my mother back. If I had more of her, then maybe I would need less of Drake. I did say maybe now. I looked up and my Momma was crying. She hugged my neck, and I left to go to school.

CHAPTER 8

It had rained all day in school, and it was still raining when school let out. When we got off at the bus stop, our mother was there waiting for us.

"How was your day girls? Did you have a good day?" she asked us as we got in the car.

"Good mommy," Gia answered.

"Are you guys hungry?" she asked.

"Yes Ma'am," we both answered in unison.

We by-passed the house and went to one of my favorite places, T.G.I.F.

As we pulled into the parking lot, I swore I saw Drake's car leaving. Not only was it Drake's car, but there was a girl in the car. If looks could kill, that nigga would be dead! I couldn't get a real good look at the girl because it was raining. But trust and believe I saw her. I had to tell myself, Destiny calm down. Destiny calm down. I was not going to let him spoil my dinner with my family. I could tell that this really meant a lot to my mom.

The food was great as usual, and we all enjoyed ourselves. Even though Drake was right there on my mind, so were my mother and sister. They meant the world to me. I was going to make an honest effort not to disappoint, or upset my mom. I know that she can't change what happened to me, and I know that it was not her fault. But I also can't change what I feel and what's in my heart. I can't go back to being the little girl that she wants me to be. That girl is long gone.

We finished our dinner, and our mother paid for the check. I can tell my mother knew something was heavy on my mind, but she didn't say anything. On our way home in the car, my sister and I thanked our mother for the dinner. She told us that every weekend we were going to get together and do something as a family. That sounded good to us. As soon as we got home Gia took her shower first, and I took mine last. We said our prayers together and got into bed. I was still too upset to call Drake. I would call him tomorrow.

The following day, it was school as usual. For some reason, it seemed like the day would never end. I was not in a good mood at all. It was finally over, and we were walking home from the bus stop. I had just put the key in, and was turning the door knob when the phone rang. After looking at the caller id I started not to answer, but I couldn't help myself.

"Hello."

"Hey Desi what's up?" asked Drake.

"Minding my business," I replied dryly.

"What's up with the attitude? What's going on with you?"

"Don't give me that bullshit. I saw you leave T.G.I.F. with some chick in your car," I said angrily.

"Wait a minute, what were you doing at T.G.I.F.?"

"Don't you try and flip this on me. I asked you a question."

"That was business, and I can't talk over this phone,"

he said.

"Yeah, whatever."

"You never told me what you were doing there."

"My mom, my sister, and I all went out to eat. It was nice," I answered.

"When can I see you? I want to catch a movie or something."

"Tomorrow is cool, but it has to be early. Maybe right after school, we need to talk."

"Okay, I'll pick you up after school."

"Talk to you later," I said as I hung up the phone.

I told my mom that I was going to get my nails done and to the mall after school. She said that it was okay, and that she would have Aunt Donna to meet Gia at the bus stop and walk her home. I did, in fact get my nails done before we caught a movie. After the movie Drake took me straight home. My mother was in her room, so I went straight to mines. I showered, lotion up, and put on my pajamas. Gia and I said our prayers and got into bed.

CHAPTER 9

The next week seemed to fly by. It was Friday before I knew it. When Gia and I came home from school, no one was there. Gia went around the corner to Rachel's house, and I called Drake to come and get me. He wanted me to dress up in the black and gold outfit that he'd just bought me. It was a black one piece halter jump suite, with a gold chain belt. I wore my gold bracelets, gold herring bone necklace, a gold clutch handbag, and my open toe gold stilettos. I was the shit. I sprayed on some Victoria's Secret body splash too, to top it off.

Drake was there in less than an hour. I walked out the door and made sure I had my keys. He got out the car and opened the passenger door for me. He was looking tight as well. My baby had on a fresh pair of Giraud jeans, a button down Polo shirt, a white tee underneath, and a new pair of Jordan's. Did I mention that the brother was smelling good? Oh my God.

"Damn baby, what's your name?" he asked as I got in the car.

"Boy stop playing," I said still smiling.

Why is it when I looked up, I saw haters peeking out of the window? He gave me a kiss before we pulled off.

We stopped at the Sport's Bar to eat and have a few

drinks, while catching some of the football game. Drake loved sports, especially football. The Tampa Bay Buccaneer's were playing the Dallas Cowboys. He had gotten so hyped up, that I got into the game. It was then that I learned about the different player positions, and what a 1st down meant.

It was eleven o'clock when we made it to his cousin's party and the party was live. It was the liveliest house party that I'd ever been too. They had a D.J., the pool area was packed, and there was plenty of food and drinks. Waitresses were all over the place. They served drinks wearing nothing but a bikini. Party decorations were everywhere. There were two dance floors, one outside in the pool area, and the other inside. This place was packed. The baller's were definitely in the building.

Drake and I had a ball! We laughed, talked and danced all night long. We were vibing in our own world. All eyes were on us as we made it to the dance floor. His cousin Mario walked up to us while we were dancing.

"What up cuz?" Mario asked.

"I can't call it. Just chilling with my lady."

"What's up Ms. Destiny? Do you mind if I get a dance?" he asked.

I looked up at Drake, to see his expression.

"If it's alright with my girl," Drake said, with that sexy cocky smile on his face.

I didn't see a problem with it, so I shook my head yes. The D.J. played *'Whoomp There It Is'* and everybody came to the dance floor. I was feeling good. It was almost two o'clock when we left the party. I was tired and sleepy. It was too late to be creeping into my house. So we left there and went straight to his mother's house, where we stayed the night. As soon as my face touched the pillow, I was fast asleep. We held each other all night.

I'm glad we left when we did though. The next morning we found out that there was a big fight over a dice game, and someone got shot. No one was arrested, and the body was found in a ditch nearby.

"Man, that's fucked up. That was my folks," Drake stated shaking his head.

"I'm just glad that it wasn't you," I replied.

I made it home the next day at 10am. Everyone was gone, except Aunt Donna. I was getting ready to take a shower and change clothes, when she asked me to have a seat on the couch. I sat down next to her, not prepared for what she was about to tell me next.

"What's up Auntie?" I asked.

"Gia is at Rachel's house, and your Momma's in jail."

"For what?" I asked.

"Possession of crack cocaine. I've already paid her bond. I'm just waiting for them to release her," she said.

I think that I went into a temporary state of shock. I could not move, or say anything for a few seconds! My mother in jail, no, no, not my Momma. I couldn't believe it. My mother had never been to jail before. I had to get up and breathe.

I went into my room, checked my stash, and then added the money that Drake had just given me. I picked out something to wear and took a shower. After getting dressed I went back in the front room with Aunt Donna.

Auntie had it going on. She was in her early thirties, with no kids. She was a very beautiful dark-skinned woman, with sharp artistic features. Her eyebrows were perfectly arched, naturally. Her high cheekbones made her look like a model. She was short, with a small waistline, a big butt, and hips. Whenever we were together somewhere, guys always tried to hit on her. On top of all that, she was cool as hell.

Auntie fired up a joint, while watching the news.

"Can I hit that?" I asked.

She looked at me and said, "I know that you smoke, because I smell it on you everyday. But you better not tell your Momma that I gave this to you."

"Aiight, that's cool."

From that moment on, Aunt Donna was my buddy. I would burn with her, and she would burn with me. I talked to her about everything. I would tell her things that I was afraid to tell my mother. She would give me advice when I needed help with something and she also put me in my place when I needed it.

My mother was released later that evening. I stayed at the house while Aunt Donna went to pick her up. When she walked in the door, there was something different about her. There was a certain reserved air around her, or humbleness in her eyes, that resonated deep in her spirit. Maybe she was embarrassed by what had happened. Maybe she felt bad as a mother. Maybe she was just tired. Maybe she was happy to be home. I don't know. Maybe it was all of the above.

"Hey Momma, I love you," I exclaimed, happy to see her.

"I love you too baby. Where's your sister?" she asked.

"She stayed the night over Rachel's house," I answered.

Aunt Donna went to her room, while my mother and I sat down and had a talk. She explained to me that she had found God, and that things were going to be a lot different. She said that she was going to become more involved in our lives.

"We are going to start going to church on Sunday's as a family. Momma's sorry for not being there lately, but all of that's gonna change. I am going to start checking over homework every night, and we are going to read bible verses before bed every evening," she said.

It sounded good at the time, but I didn't realize how much of a change that it actually meant. She called Rachel's house and had her mother to bring Gia home. That Sunday morning we all got up, and dressed for church, even Aunt Donna.

The next few weeks were okay, but I was not feeling this change. I hardly saw Drake, and I couldn't smoke. Lord, I need a blunt bad. The only chance that I got to smoke was when Aunt Donna came home. I had to sneak to smoke even then. This was not going to work. Something had to give. We attended church on Sunday mornings, Sunday nights, Wednesday night bible study, and Friday night youth meetings.

I would sneak out of the window at night to see Drake. My attendance at school dropped. The more restrictions she put on me, the more I bucked. She worked during the day, and started taking nursing classes at night. I was glad. During her school hours is when I got a chance to see Drake. This went on for some months. I made sure he gave me enough weed to last me through the week.

CHAPTER 10

The school year was quickly approaching an end and Gia and I would again be advancing to the next grade. I was ready for the summer to begin. Our neighborhood came to life in the summer and the park was always crunk. There were block parties in the evenings and I met a lot of people from hanging with Drake. I was known and respected for being Drake's Lady. It was going to be a good summer break.

It was the last day of school, and my mother had just made it home from work. I had just smoked a blunt, and was checking out music videos on BET when she walked in.

"Well hello young lady," she said.

"Hey Ma."

"Guess what? I have some good news and some bad news. Which one do you want first?" she asked.

"Give me the good news first."

"I found us a nice three bedroom, two and ½ bathroom house across town. It's perfect, I know you're gonna love it! The bad news is, I can't pick up the keys for another two weeks. But that's okay. That gives us plenty of time to pack," she said excitedly.

"Do what? I like this house. I like my friends, and I like my school. I don't want to move Momma," I complained.

"It's a better house, better school, and better neighborhood. You'll meet new friends. We are moving, it's not negotiable, so you need to start packing," she said.

I was both mad and depressed. I didn't want to move away from my baby. This was my first love. I was his queen. She was doing this on purpose. I went in my room and called Drake to tell him the news.

"Calm down Desi, it's okay. It doesn't matter where you move, I'll be there. You know that I can't let you get away from me that easy," he said teasing.

He knew just how to make me feel better.

The two weeks had passed by quick and we moved into the new place. I hated it already. It was a nice house, but it was a boring neighborhood. I didn't see any black people around, and I heard that the school was boring too. I was going crazy. I needed to see my baby.

Just like he promised, he would come and get me on nights my mother had to go to school. We still went to the movies, and out to eat. I would sneak out of the window at night when my mother was asleep, and return home early in the morning before it was time for her to get ready for work. Nothing was gonna keep me away from Drake.

One night he was supposed to pick me up and I waited up all night long for him. There was no Drake. I called his phone all night long and it kept going straight to voicemail. Where the hell was he? We had planned this all day! I finally fell asleep after tossing and turning all night. The next day I called his phone again.

"Hello," answered Mario

"Where's Drake?" I asked a little angered.

"He got locked up last night," replied Mario.

"He what?" I asked in disbelief.

"Yeah, he served an informant, and they got him," said Mario.

"What does he need to get out?" I asked.

"He doesn't have a bond. This phone is gonna be disconnected, so you can call his Momma if you need anything. More than likely, they're gonna send him up the road," he said.

I was speechless.

Then he said to me, "You know that I have had my eye on you, what's up?"

CLICK.

Now that was some real shady shit. Drake is his blood cousin and he knows better than that. BUSTER.

My man was gone. The police took him away from me. Broken hearted, I cried all day long. He wasn't coming to pick me up. What did I do to deserve this? I needed a blunt bad and Aunt Donna wasn't around, she was at her man's house most of the time in those days. I knew that every neighborhood had a weed man though; I just needed to find him.

As the days passed by, I started to get out more and learn my area. There was another black family around the corner and I saw a girl about my age outside watching her little sister ride her bicycle. I walked over and introduced myself.

"Hi, my name is Destiny, and I just moved around the corner," I said with an extended hand.

"I'm Jasmine, and that's my sister Raisa," she replied.

She was a cute brown-skinned girl with a neat slim shape, and she had on the latest designer clothes. I especially liked her shoes, they were hot. I wondered where she got those from. She seemed like she would know where the weed man was. So I asked her.

"Is there anything to do around here? What do you do for fun?"

"There's not much to do around here, but I hang out at the skating rink. It's always crunk on Sunday nights. The beach is live too on Sunday's. Everybody who's somebody is there," she stated.

"Word?"

"Girl, that shit is always crunk. Nigga's be riding around showing their cars, and splurging all day. My homeboy is picking me up this weekend, you can ride if you want to," she said.

"Do you smoke?" I asked.

"Oh, hell yeah. Let me take my little sister in the house. We can walk around the corner and smoke," she said.

Thank you Lord, I found a kindred soul. Jasmine was a year older than me, and we had a lot in common. We both like to dress in the latest fashions, we both like to have a good time, and we both liked money.

Jasmine and I hung out all the time. We went to the movies on Friday nights, the skating rink on Saturdays, and the beach on Sundays. She would stay the night at my house almost every weekend and we got around everywhere. She only dated the baller's, and they got us into the hottest clubs, 21 and older and VIP. I began meeting lots of people, and going to places I had never even heard of. We would have guys over to the house while my mother was at school or work too.

I still had the money stash that Drake had given me. Some of it was spent, but I was still straight. I had to come up with a master plan. I loved to shop too much, and being broke was not an option. Instead of going broke, I would go into the mall and steal what I wanted. Most of the people in the stores already knew me. I was a frequent shopper. The more I did it, the easier it became. It soon became a habit. I would have a pocket full of money, and still take what I wanted. I would get stuff for me, Jasmine, and my sister. Jasmine had unofficially become my first customer. Sometimes she paid me, most of the time I gave it to her for free. We did each other favors in different ways. She had my back, and I had hers. I started stealing beer and liquor from the corner store, just for practice. I was actually pretty good.

My mother had graduated from school as a LPN, and had already been offered a position at a local hospital. She worked the overnight shift. Her hours were from 10pm – 10am. Like B.G. of Cash Money says, 'Oh it's On Now'. I didn't have to sneak out of the window at night anymore, I could walk straight out the front door.

Jasmine couldn't hang out like I could, because she couldn't stay with me every night. So my friend base expanded. The more people that I met, the easier it became for me to get into any club, 21 and over. I dressed my ass off, kept money in my pocket, and carried myself better than some grown women. I knew how to make a man give me what I wanted, without laying on my back for it, and I was only 14 years old.

I met a guy named D-man in a club one night. This brother had it going on. He was grilled out and I'm a sucker for a nigga with a tight grill. He dressed nice too and smelled good. He was hitting all the right spots. I was standing at the bar, waiting on my drink when he walked over to me.

"What's up Lil' Momma?" he asked.

"Just chilling," I said.

"Damn, you looking good. What are you drinking on?" he asked while checking me out.

"Apple Martini."

"I got you. What's your name? Put your number in my phone," he said handing me his phone.

We were exchanging numbers when the bartender returned with my drink. Dude was pretty cool. I learned that he was from Miami, and 23yrs old. He said that he had a house here and Miami, and that he was always back and forth. I liked his style, and how he carried himself. He was definitely a keeper.

Over the next few weeks, D-man and I kicked it a lot. We had fun together, but there was a very serious side to him. The more I was around him, the better I got to know him. Slowly, I was being exposed to his world, and his business operations. He didn't play when it came to his money, and he was very careful about the moves he made.

After dating for a couple of months, he finally invited me to his house. It was a huge 4 bedroom, 2 ½ bath split-level home with a pool. It was very clean and nicely decorated.

"This is nice. Do you live here by yourself," I asked?

"No. I have a roommate. She is more like a business partner/Big sister," he said.

"This is a lot of space."

"Come on, I'll introduce you and show you around."

In the family room is where I met his big sister. Her name was Lacy. Now she was a Boss Chick, for real. D-man and his click would bring in major weight. Lacy had the connections, and knew who needed work. She

69

bought her own weight for the lo-lo, and would set them up with the right people. Lacy and I clicked immediately. I started hanging over there all the time. Even when D-man was out of town, Lacy would come and get me.

Lacy and I became hella cool. She had two kids. A 6yr old girl, and a 5yr old boy. They were both crazy about me. I would play with them, and make them laugh. I'd cook them things to eat, and sometimes give them a bath. Lacy had taken me under her wing. She schooled me on everything about the game, all the way down to the hustlers. She taught me that nothing's for free, and that everything had a price.

D-man and I still had not slept together. That didn't matter though, because he still threw me money on the regular. Lacy told me that the longer you make a man wait, the more that he would do for you to get it. He always made sure that I was straight before he went out of town. I really didn't have time to miss him, because Lacy and I were everywhere. She took me to my mother's house so that I could get all of my clothes. I knew that my mother was at work because I didn't see her car in the driveway.

"I'll be right back," I told Lacy as I got out of the car.

When I walked in the house, Gia was on the couch watching television.

"Are you here to stay? Momma's been looking for you," she stated.

"No, I'm moving out. Tell Momma that I'm sorry and that I love her, but I can't stay here anymore," I said.

"What do you mean, you're moving out? What about me?" she asked.

"You know that you're my baby girl, and that I love

you. But, I can't take you where I'm going. I'm still here whenever you need me, all you have to do is call me. I'll be right there," I answered.

"Are you going to be okay? There are crazy people out there."

I smiled. My little sister was actually worried about me.

"I'm a big girl, I'll be just fine."

I went into my room and packed all of my things, including my personal items. I gave my sister $500 and told her to put it up.

"Don't spend this money at all, unless it's an emergency. If you need anything, anything at all, just call me. When Momma gives you your allowance save it, don't spend it. As long as you have something put up, you will never be broke," I told her.

"Okay. I love you," she said.

"I love you back," I said as I walked out the front door.

CHAPTER 11

I had officially moved in with Lacy and D-man. She was like the big sister that I never had. She was 25yrs old, and everyone thought that I was 17. We had a ball together. We went back and forth to Miami on the regular. Sometimes it was to shop, and sometimes it was on a business trip. I had never seen so much dope and money at one time in my life.

The money that I was making taking these trips, I didn't even have to touch. I was still spending D-man's money. I always put my money up. Drake taught me that. There would be times when Lacy would go somewhere for a few hours, and she would drop me two or three hundred dollars just for being there at the house with the kids. D-man always brought me gifts back from Miami. He always surprised me with something different. I guess that you could say that we were officially a couple now. He was the only man that I dealt with. He made me laugh, and took care of me. While he was gone, I waited anxiously for him to return.

Periodically, I would call my mom. I just wanted to let her know that I was okay. She heard my voice at least every other week. She went from pleading with me to come home, to just wanting to make sure that I was okay. She knew that I was not a naïve little girl.

It had been five months since I'd left home. I had a nice amount of money stashed. My wardrobe had tripled, and I was doing what I wanted to do, when I wanted to do it. I guess it's true when they say 'All good things come to an end'. One of D-man's homies in the click got pulled over while making a run. The nigga snitched on the whole click, even Lacy. She was indicted by the FEDS for conspiracy. I called her sister to pick me and the kids up when they got her. I barely had time to pack my things and the kid's things because her sister made it there in less than twenty minutes.

Lacy wound up being sentenced to 25yrs FED time. The fucked up part about is, those same nigga's had to testify against her in court and point her out while on the witness stand. They charged her with Conspiracy. Her mother obtained custody of the kids and that was the last time I ever saw Lacy again.

Her sister's name was Kya and she already knew me from hanging out with Lacy. She was cool and also crazy. This chick was a straight hustler too. I guess it ran in their blood. She sold drugs here and there, but no major weight. Her thing was boosting. It was a click of seven, including me. We started at eight in the morning, when the stores opened. We went out of town, to all of the outlet malls, and the big department stores to boost. We were a team of real professionals. By the end of the day, we had everything from personal hygiene products, hair products, household products, and jewelry; to every single name brand clothing that was out there. By the time we made it home, everyone had garbage bags full of shit.

Every hustler on the Southside placed orders with us.
They shopped for themselves, their girlfriends, and their
kids. My hairdo was paid up in advance for months. My
stylist had every product that she needed. All I had to do
was call and schedule the appointment.

Whenever we weren't shopping, we hit all of the hot
spots, the entire crew. The crew consisted of me, Kya,
Tammy, Asia, Bernice, Pam, and Gretta. Everybody was
crazy in their own way. Tammy and I were the only two
that didn't have any kids, so we hung out the most. We
stayed in the flyest gear, and everyone knew and
respected us. I was enjoying myself and living life in the
fast lane.

One day the whole crew was together working as
usual in the Cordova Mall shopping. It was just the same
routine, a different day. This particular day though, I
branched off from the crew. That was not unusual. We
all did our thugism, but eventually we hooked back up. I
noticed a white man following me around in the store. I
didn't give a damn, he didn't see me take shit. I'm me,
he can't touch me I thought. So, I proceeded to walk out
the store to the car. Fuck, why is he still behind me, I
asked myself? As I walked across the parking lot, I saw
three other officer's in uniform heading towards me.
Damn. I'm caught. I had a bag full of shit, and shit in
my girdle I couldn't ditch. I was taken to the security
office and asked all kinds of information. I fed them so
much bogus shit, I started believing it myself. I was
barred from the mall, placed in handcuffs, and taken to
the Juvenile Justice Center. I couldn't believe that shit.
We were supposed to be going to the club that night.
Fuck that, I ain't going to jail. While in the back of the
car, I somehow managed to get the cuffs from behind my

back, by sliding my body through my arms, and bringing my hands to the front while still in the cuffs. As soon as the officer pulled up in front of the detention center and opened the back door, I jetted. I took off running in hand cuffs and all. It was dark, and had started to rain. I looked back to see his fat ass was far behind me. I was still determined to make it to the club, but how the hell was I gonna get those cuffs off, I asked myself. I was still running, but now in a residential area. Then all off a sudden, I saw blue lights everywhere; in front of me, behind me, and on both my sides. Damn. They got me, Fuck. They took me back to the detention center and booked me; under a fake name of course. I had them to call one of my home girls that was over 21yrs old and told them that my parents were out of town. All of my people knew the drill. And I still made it to the club. Those people couldn't fuck with me.

I had heard that my mother was looking for me around town. I avoided her at all costs and by any means necessary. I had a juvenile warrant for my arrest for shoplifting; hell, I had several warrants out in different names. Whenever I got jammed up, someone would come get me, and I would never return to court. Eventually, my mother found out about all of this. I knew that she would have me locked up, just to get me off the streets. She was going to the spots that she thought I hung out in. People from Wedgewood and Ensley would tell me when my mother was looking for me. My crew and I were kind of everywhere; we didn't stay in one particular place, so it was hard for her to catch up with me. She did find out Kya's first and last name though, and she knew that's who I lived with.

Kya and I were out and about one day, trying to make

some money. We had gotten rid of all the merchandise that we had, and didn't have time to shop for more. It was her son's birthday, and we were throwing a big party for him. Kya was going all out for this party and wanted to make some of her money back. We rode around the hood for a minute. No one seemed to be hanging out.

"Damn, it really is dry out here. They say nobody has any hard on this side of town," Kya said.

"Ain't nobody doing nothing on the speed bump road? Somebody gotta be straight over there," I asked.

"Nope, they are dry over there too. They've been shopping with nigga's on the Westside."

"Don't Berniece's baby daddy, Lil' Bean serve?" I asked.

"Yeah, let's ride. I need to holla at Bernice anyhow."

I rolled a blunt and turned the music up. We jammed the whole way there listening to *Dr. Dre's 'Ain't Nothing But a G Thang'*. It had been a long time since I was on the Westside. It used to be Drake's stomping grounds and riding through the neighborhood brought back so many memories. I wondered if Drake's mom still lived out that way. I wondered how he was doing. No one would ever take his place.

It was mid afternoon when we pulled into Berniece's driveway. She lived in a cozy three bedroom house and the inside was decked out. She was always shopping, with or without the crew. I loved the way she had her crib set up. I still don't understand how she kept her white furniture so clean, especially with three small kids in the house. I saw when she opened the curtains as we pulled into the driveway.

"What's up?" she yelled as she answered the door. "Come on in. Do ya'll want something to drink? I just made a pitcher of frozen margaritas," she said as we followed her into the kitchen.

The bitch loved to get her drink on. No matter what time of the day, she was always sipping on something. We helped ourselves to glasses, and poured our own drinks.

"Are you coming to Jamel's party," Kya asked?

"Yeah, I'm waiting for Lil' Bean to get back from picking the kids up, plus he gotta stop by his brother's house," Bernice replied.

"Speaking of Lil' Bean, do you know if he's straight? I need to buy some work," Kya asked.

"Nope, not yet. He was waiting for his peoples around the corner to get back. We can ride over there if ya'll want. He's pretty cool with me too. I need to stop by Bang's house anyhow. She lives up the street from one of his spots," Bernice said.

Bernice called Lil' Bean before we left the house.

"What's up?" he answered.

"Did you holla at your peoples around the corner?" she asked.

"Yeah, I'm straight. I gotta make a few plays, but I'll be home in a couple of hours."

"Kya need to holla at him too. Let him know we're on our way."

"Alright, I'll see you in a minute."

"Bye," Bernice said hanging up the phone.

We grabbed our purses, and headed for the door.

The spot was four streets over, so still in walking distance; even though we drove. There were two guys standing in front of the door as we pulled into the driveway.

"Is Mario here?" Bernice asked one of the guys.

"Who are you?" he asked peeping in the car.

"This is Bernice."

"Oh, you folks, he's in there," the guy answered.

We got out the car and walked in the house. I wondered if the Mario in question was Drake's cousin Mario. I guess I was about to find out. Kya and I sat on the sofa, while Bernice went straight to the back of the house. She returned five minutes later and sat next to us.

"What's up?" Kya asked.

"You're good. He's finishing up something," Bernice answered.

Just as she said that, he walked into the front room and sat on the love seat. Hell yeah, it was Mario's bitch ass. For some reason, I couldn't stand that nigga. It wasn't only because he tried to holla at me when Drake got locked up, there was just something about him that I just didn't like.

"What's up Destiny? Long time, long see ma," he said, interrupting my thoughts.

"Yeah, I know."

"I see you still looking good."

I ignored him. Buster.

"You look familiar. Didn't you used to be over Lacy's house?" he asked Kya.

"That's my sister," Kya replied.

"Get the hell out of here. D-man used to be my boy. I heard what happened, that was fucked up man," he replied.

"Yeah, I know."

They exchanged a few more pleasantries, and walked to the back. Ten minutes later, Mario was walking all of us to the door.

"Have you heard from Drake?" I asked just before

walking out of the door.

"Not in a minute. He used to call."

"How much time does he have to serve? Do you have his address?"

"He'll do five years. I don't have his address here, but I will get it and give it to Bernice if you want," he said.

"Alright."

Damn, five years. I guess it could be a lot worse. Lacy and D-Man got twenty-five years.

After dropping Bernice off, we headed back to Wedgewood. We posted up on the block with the half ounce she bought and she was the only one who had some hard in the whole neighborhood. It didn't take long before she completely sold out and the junkies were still looking for her. It was time to go and get dressed for the party.

Everyone and their kids showed up. The kids had a ball, and of course the adults were partying hard too. There was a spades game going on, and the music was blasting. People were dancing to *Will Smith's 'Summertime'* with their red cups in their hands. The food was plentiful and everybody enjoyed themselves. Jamel had toys for days. It reminded me of my 10th birthday party, but I had to quickly change my thoughts. I didn't want to remember the horrible part of that night. Nervously, I scanned the crowd, just to make sure that the strange man from in front of the corner store was nowhere in sight.

Two months had passed since Jamel's party. The kids had just left for school, and Kya and I both went back to sleep. I dozed off on the couch while watching the news and Kya was in her bedroom asleep. I heard someone yell "Police", and then a loud 'boom'. I jumped straight up. The police had kicked in the door and was standing right over me. Kya walked into the living room, wearing her house robe to see what's going on.

"Kya Dennis, place your hands in the air," they yelled.

Their guns were drawn and aimed, ready to shoot. They had a no-knock warrant.

"You are under arrest for sale and delivery of crack cocaine," one of the officers said.

She was cuffed and escorted to the police car.

"Take my kids to my Momma house," she yelled before getting into the back of the car.

I couldn't stop the tears from falling down my face. The officers asked me my name and relationship to her. I gave them a fake name, and told them that I was her niece. I called Bernice to come and get me while they were searching the house for any additional drugs. They didn't find anything. Nothing. They tore the house up. I could not believe that this was happening, again. Why does the police take away everybody that I love? I hate the police.

As if this wasn't enough, it got worse. Somehow my mother finds out that Kya was locked up and she went to file another charge on her, Interference with Custody; which is a felony. I felt awful. Kya didn't even know my real age. She was given a bond on the drug charges, but not on the custody charge. Her kids were at her mother's house. Her mother is one hell of a woman because she already had Lacy's two kids, plus she now had Kya's three too. I moved all of my things over to Asia's house, which is Kya's niece. The next few weeks are hectic for everybody.

I kept calling my mother, trying to get her to drop the charges. If she dropped them, then Kya could bond out.

"Momma, please drop the charges. She has small kids that need her," I pleaded.

"I have a child that I love, and am responsible for. She didn't send my child home. She didn't tell you that you need to be in school. She didn't tell you to go home, because your mother might be worried about you. Instead, she was driving you around town so that you can shoplift," she said angrily.

"Momma, I was stealing way before I met her. And, she can't tell me what to do. She can't 'make' me go home, or to school. If I wasn't at her house, I would be somewhere else," I said.

"I'm not dropping anything. She needs to accept responsibility for her actions."

I got so pissed off when she said that. I just went off! I cussed my mother out. This was the very first time I ever talked to my mother like that. I mean, I went off on her, then hung up.

Two days later, I received a phone call from Jasmine at 7:00am in the morning. What the hell could she possibly want this early?

"Yeah," I answered with an attitude.

"Get up, and get dressed. I am on my way to pick you up," Jasmine said.

"Girl, are you crazy? What do you want?"

"Bitch just get up and get dressed," she said and hung up.

She knew exactly where I was because we still talked all the time and within 30 minutes, she pulled up in front of Asia's apartment.

Jumping in the car I asked, "What's up Jasmine? Why are you pulling me out of the bed this early?"

She had tears in her eyes.

"What's wrong?"

"Let's wait until we get to the house," she answered.

The tears were now falling down her face. I didn't know what to think. We rode the entire ride in silence.

When we pulled up in her yard, I saw two police cars. I froze up.

"Bitch, you trying to set me up?" I asked ready to go the fuck off.

"No, no, it's nothing like that."

When we walked into the house, I saw my little sister sitting on the couch. She was crying and screaming.

"What's wrong with her? What's wrong with her?" I yelled!

A white female police officer pulled me to the side.

"Can you please have a seat?" she asked

"No. I'd rather stand. What's going on?"

"I am sorry to be the one to tell you, but your mother passed away last night," she said.

No term in any dictionary could possibly explain what I felt. My mother and sister were all that I had. It had always been just the three of us. My mother was more than my mother, she was my father too.

We were all each other had.

I love my mother. She was a strong, independent black woman, and mother. I know that I hadn't been treating her right, but I always thought that when I was tired of running the streets, I would go back home. I never made it home. I would never see her smile again. Then I thought about the last conversation that I had with her, cussing her out. I fell to my knees, crying uncontrollably. Jasmine walked over and hugged me, rocking me back and forth.

"Lord no, not my Momma."

Why has God taken away everybody that I love? My sister was all I had left. Maybe God was teaching me how to take care of myself, and preparing me for the journey that lay ahead. Maybe everything that I've gone through so far has been to make me stronger. I had book smarts, and street smarts. I knew how to hustle, and had game out of this world. Whatever it was, I still needed my mother. No one can ever truly understand or comprehend how you feel when you lose a mother, no matter what they say, unless they have lost a mother too.

It felt like I died with her. I was empty and dead on the inside. It was like I was just walking around numb with no feelings at all. I didn't care about no one, or nothing. My attitude was like fuck it. It's whatever.

CHAPTER 12

The next few days were crazy. My grandmother came to Florida to have my mother's body shipped back to Mississippi and she obtained all the important and necessary documents. My mother had a life insurance policy through the hospital which only covered her funeral expenses. Grandma paid to have a truck load and ship everything in our house to Mississippi.

The funeral was scheduled for the following week. A bus load of Momma's church members came up to pay their respects. Everything seemed so unreal to me. I mean, I was at the funeral looking at her body, but something in my mind refused to let it register that she was not coming back. I didn't shed a tear. I know it's crazy, but it's true. I think that I was in some sort of denial.

After the funeral everyone went to grandmother's house to eat. Family had come in from everywhere. People that I had never seen before, or even heard of. Everyone came by to send their condolences.

I have one aunt that's the motor mouth of the family. Her name is Elena. I couldn't stand the bitch. I never did like her. She always thought that she was God's gift to the earth because she was high yellow. She's the one that always kept up the messiness in the family and she was the one that you heard before you see. I was sitting in the front room with my sister and I heard her all the way from the kitchen.

"That's a shame, you know that she didn't even cry at her own mother's funeral," she told one of my distant cousins.

Before I knew it, I was in the kitchen in her face.

"You don't know me like that! You better keep my name out your mouth," I yelled!

The whole house got quiet.

"See, I told you that she was disrespectful."

All I remember is one of my uncles trying to pull me off of her, while she was blocking her face on the ground.

My uncle took me outside to get some air. I stayed out there talking to one of my uncle friends, trying to calm down.

"You smoke?" Robert asked.

"Hell yeah! I need to get away from here," I answered.

We hopped in his ride and left. We rode around for a couple of hours just chilling. I needed to get my mind away from everything that was going on. This wasn't happening to me. I felt like a viewer, screening a movie.

"Here is my number. If you need anything, call me," he said as we pulled into my grandmother's driveway.

Almost a week had passed since the funeral, and I was going crazy. This is definitely not me. I could not stay, or live in Mississippi. I see why my mother left. I'd left most of my clothes at Asia's house. I knew that I was going back to Florida.

What I hated the most was the fact that I had to leave my sister behind. There was no way that I could take her where I was going. I couldn't have her in the environment that I was in. I had to leave her behind. I sat Gia down and tried to explain to her that I did not get along with the people in grandma's house.

"Gia, I can't stay here. I'm sorry for leaving you here, but I gotta go. Please don't be mad at me," I asked her.

"You promise to come back and get me?" she asked.

"You already know that. As soon as I'm able, I promise I will."

"I love you Destiny."

"I love you back baby girl."

She hugged my neck, and we held on to each other for awhile. I made sure that she had several contact numbers for me. I packed my small luggage bag, gave her a few hundred dollars, and walked out of the front door in the middle of the night.

I walked three blocks down to the nearby corner store. Robert better answer this damn phone, I thought. He finally picked up on the forth ring.

"Hello," he answered sleepily.

"This is Destiny, I need a ride."

"Right now, where are you?"

"I'm at the gas station right around the corner from the house. Can you come now and get me?"

"Stay where you're at, I'll be right there," he replied hanging up the phone.

Robert was handsome. Usually, I wasn't attracted to light skinned guys, but he had a sexy swag about himself. He was grilled up, top and bottom, tall, and lean. What stood out the most to me was his realness. He was a straight up type of cat. He didn't care who he offended, he called it like he saw it. I liked that.

He pulled up in an old school Cadillac, with the music turned all the way down. He didn't want my family, especially my uncles, who he hustled with, to know that he was trying to get with their little niece. I didn't have to lie about my age, he already knew. Again, my personality, my age, my mentality, and my physical appearance did not match up. I guess wrong is wrong. He was in his early twenties and I was only 15yrs old. If he didn't say anything, then I wouldn't.

We stopped to get something to eat and got a hotel. The following morning he dropped me off at the Greyhound Bus station.

"Here's a little something to put in your pocket," he said handing me a wad of cash.

"Thank you. Can you do me another favor? Can you look out for my little sister, and keep those young boys away from her.? Just make sure she's straight," I asked.

"I'll look out for your lil' sister," he said.

"Call me when you get to Florida. If you ever need anything, just call."

"I will."

I grabbed my bag and disappeared in the bus station. I purchased my ticket and sat waiting for my bus to arrive. I was outta there!

I called Asia from the bus station in Mississippi to let her know what time I would get back to Florida. She was there waiting on me as soon as I arrived.

"Bitch, please tell me that you have a cigarette?" I asked as I got into the car.

"Yeah, I'm sorry about your moms," she said genuinely.

"Thanks."

I know that she meant well, but she didn't understand how I felt. I was in this dog-eat-dog world all by myself. Me against the World. There was no crutch to lean on, no one to take care of me, no one to depend on but myself.

CHAPTER 13

The next few months, I was strictly on a paper chase. Fuck the clubs, and fuck going out. Anything that had to do with making some money, I wanted in. I would buy ounces of weed, trying to flip my money. I bought two – three hundred dollars worth of hard at a time trying to double my money. I was still taking orders, boosting clothes. Sometimes I shopped with the crew, sometimes I shopped by myself. I got my hair done so much, that I knew how to do certain styles. I was doing hair in Asia's kitchen on the regular. Anything to make that extra dollar. I got mad love from the players on the block. Everyone knew and respected my hustle. Nigga's knew if they stepped to me, they had to come correct.

Of all the hustlers that tried to step to me, one caught my eye. His name is Keston. Ole boy was black as hell, just the way I like it; grilled up with mad flavor. The way that he carried himself commanded respect. He came to the house with one of his boys to buy some green. He smelled good and looked good. That's what caught my attention. He saw me checking him out.

"Can I holla at you for a minute?" he asked.

"What's up?"

"I need a quarter bag, and your phone number," he said.

"Sorry, my number is not for sale."

"Are you sure about that? I always get what I want."

"We'll see," I answered with a smirk on my face.

He paid me, I served him, and they left.

Asia was getting ready for work.

"What you know about dude?" I asked her.

"I know that both of them are from the Westside. They be at one of Mario's spots," she answered.

"I don't care for that nigga Mario."

"Me either. He has a lot of women and they say that he be chopping people head off with his prices. Plus, he uses too much cut on his work," she said.

"That nigga is something serious. He's making more money off less work," I replied.

"Guess who he's creeping with?" she asked.

"Who?"

"I said guess," she said impatiently.

"Hell, I don't know! Just tell me," I yelled!

"Bernice."

"Stop lying! Lil' Bean will break her back," I replied in disbelief.

"That nigga is shady. He be all up in Lil' Bean's face, serving him and everything, and knocking off his girl," Asia said.

"I knew it was a reason that I didn't care for him! He tried to holla at me when Drake got locked up and that's his first cousin!"

"I don't know what Bernice see in him," said Asia.

"If Mario and Keston are cool like that, then I don't know if I want to holla at him"

"Mario is a business man. He knows damn near everybody on the Westside. I think that you should give him a chance, and see what he's talking about."

The next few weeks were like a whirlwind. Keston was very persistent. He shopped with me everyday, until I gave him my number. He turned out to be a real gentleman. He wined and dined me. We went on lots of road trips, and spent lots of time together. This seemed to soothe the pain that I felt from my mother's death. When the both of us were not working, we were inseparable. It was cool at first, and I was enjoying being catered to again. Eventually, it was starting to get old. We were around each other a little too much. It began to affect my business.

He would always say, "Don't worry about it ma, I got you."

That didn't mean shit to me, I wanted my own money. Yeah, he took care of me, and bought me nice things, but it wasn't nothing that I wasn't already doing for myself. He would pay my half of the rent at Asia's place and give me anything else that I needed. The more he did for me, the more possessive he became of me. I was not feeling this.

Every dude that came over to buy something, he would swear that I was sleeping with him. I am a business woman, and half of my customers are men! You couldn't tell him that though. He was too jealous. We would fight if he came over and guys were at the house. I had to straighten him out.

"Nigga for one, this is not my house and I don't live here alone. For two, if you are that fucking concerned, then put me in my own place! If we don't have trust, then we ain't got shit. For three, every time you ask nigga's about me, you never hear anything but real shit!"

Our arguments turned into fights. He started putting his hands on me and we would go at it. Sometimes I would have a black eye, or busted lip. I would never say what happened, but everyone knew. My friends would all tell me,

"Girl, he wouldn't put his hands on me like that. That's not love. You need to have his ass locked up!"

I don't believe in calling the police. I hate the police. Someone had to get shot, or was dying before I called the police. I wanted to get out but I just didn't know how. Every time I tried to break it off, he would do something really nice and tell me how sorry he was.

Keston swore all of my friends were whores too. He would call me a trick-or-treat because he said that I was tricking him, and treating them other nigga's. This man was crazy. What the hell had I gotten myself into? He said that he loves me, but love is not supposed to feel like that.

CHAPTER 14

It was a hot, Saturday afternoon and Asia had just made it home from work. I was doing a quick weave for this chick named Alicia. She wanted long crimps, with waterfalls at the top. The three of us talked and smoked while I did her hair. I always worked better when I was high. For some reason, it made me pay more attention to details. Someone was knocking on the door.

"I'll get it," Asia said as she passed the blunt.

"Who is it," she asked?

"Star."

Asia peeked out of the peek hole, and answered the door.

"What's up? Do ya'll have any trees," Star asked?

"Yeah, have a seat."

She took a seat on the sofa. I kept staring at her. This chick looked very familiar. I just couldn't put my finger on it. I guess she saw the puzzled look on my face, she walked into the kitchen and introduced herself.

"My name is Star. Lil' Mark from around the corner sent me."

Then I figured it out!

"Do you know a dude named Drake," I asked her?

It was the chick in the car with him at T.G.I.F. My blood was starting to boil.

"Yeah, that's my homeboy," she answered.

She now had my full attention. I sat the curling iron out of the hot stove, and stepped away from the table.

"You're the one that I saw with him at Mario's party. He used to talk about you all the time," she said.

"How did you know him," I quizzed.

"Drake used to buy a lot of work from my uncle, and sometimes I brought it to him."

"I miss my baby."

"You know who set him up, right," she asked?

"No, who?"

"His lame ass cousin Mario. That nigga is a straight up snitch, an informant."

"What?" Asia and I both asked.

"He's foul. We don't fool with him at all. He's the one who set those Miami nigga's up, and the reason Kya's door got kicked in."

"How do you know that?" asked Asia

"My uncle gets all of his information firsthand. He has a dirty cop on his payroll. That's why he's been around so long," Star said.

"But why would he do that to his own cousin," I asked?

"Because he was jealous of Drake. Drake was well known and respected. He treated people right, and he was fair. Mario always tried to get over on people, and burned a lot of bridges."

By this time, Asia was pacing the floor. Both of her aunts were locked up, all because of Mario's snitch ass!

"When was the last time you heard from Drake," I asked Star?

"My uncle talks to him all the time. Drake is like a son to him. He did everything that he could to help him out. That's why he's only serving five years."

"That nigga gotta pay for this shit," Asia said angrily.

"Here, hit the blunt Asia," I said passing it.

She needed something.

"Do you wanna hit this," I asked Star while firing up another blunt.

We all smoked and talked while I finished Alicia's hair. Star bought two quarter bags of weed, one for her, and another for Lil' Mark.

Star and I became tight after that. Everybody on the block knew her and her folks. She served soft, and I had everything else. Between the two of us, it was a one-stop shop. I had even started buying work from her uncle, and cooking up my own shit. We hung around each other all the time. I was at her house more than Asia's house lately. She lived by herself, and had no kids. Keston was not felling this at all. The more I hung out with Star, the angrier he got.

He would pop up at Star's house, trying to catch something. I was sick of his shit. One day he came over with that bullshit, while Star's uncle was there. Wrong move. Debo was an old school cat that no one played with. I stepped out of the door to talk to him. I didn't want him to embarrass me by kicking my ass in front of her uncle. On top of that, we were handling business. Keston wanted to know who was in the house, and whose car was in the driveway. We were yelling and arguing in front of the house. I was trying to keep him quiet and calm him down. This was a laid back neighborhood, and I didn't want to draw any unnecessary attention.

"You need to leave with all of that noise. I told you to call before you come by anyhow," I told him.

My words were not completely out of my mouth

before he smacked me right in my face. He hit me so hard that I stumbled back. Not two seconds later, Debo was out of the door. He beat the shit out of Keston. I felt kind of sorry for him.

"Get the fuck away from here, and don't come back," Debo yelled!

He didn't come back either. Occasionally, he would call, but I never picked up. That was a wrap.

Gradually, I moved in with Star. We balled from sun up, to sun down. She had a friend named La'Mica that she grew up with. La'Mica and I became cool too, even she didn't like me at first. She was cool, but she was a sneaky bitch. You never knew what she was up to.

La'Mica was a tall, slim, pretty and light skinned chick. I usually didn't get along with light skinned chicks, but she was kind of different. She grew up in a nice, religious household, and she was raised by both of her parents. She was accustomed to nice things. I don't really think that she knew what it meant to live in the hood. By looking at her, you would think that she was a quiet, innocent girl. Never judge a book by its cover. La'Mica is off the chain. This bitch would cuss you out in a minute! She worked in the mall part-time, and went to the Jr. College part-time. Anything about making some money, she was always down. She loved to kick it just as much as we did. What I loved the most about her was that she was smart, and she didn't give a damn. She would tell you just like it is. This bitch was 18yrs old.

Star is dark and lovely. She had long, thick, pretty hair, and was very attractive. She was the laid back one. As long as her money was right, she could shop when she wanted too, and the smoke was in the air, then she was straight. She could chump you off, and make you feel like shit without even raising her voice. On top of that, everyone knew, and respected her family. Star was the peacemaker of the group. She was 19 years old.

We would hit the interstate, and just ride out. We went to different cities and towns, clubbing. We didn't have to know shit about the areas, we would always find the hot spots. From Pensacola, to Mobile, to Mississippi, to New Orleans, it was whatever. We even went to Jacksonville, balling out of control like that was our city. One year we went to Freak Nic in Atlanta, Ga. That was one of our best trips. We tried to go someplace almost every weekend. Balling was an understatement! You got three bad chicks in one spot, at the same mother-fucking time. Man, we were hell.

When we weren't clubbing, it was all about the paper chase. I was still boosting, selling weed, and doing hair on the side. I only served hard to a select few who wanted weight. Everyone knew that Star had the best soft in town. Her phone stayed ringing. We hung around each other so much, that we began calling each other sisters. I would go with her to her parent's house for dinner, and her little sisters would call me for advice. This made me miss my family and my sister.

A year and a half had passed since my mother died and I had to leave my sister behind. I missed both of them. Every time I would hear one of my mother's favorite songs, I would get depressed. Before she passed, while I still lived with her, she loved *Gerald Levert's 'Baby Hold On To Me'*! Even though she was saved and only listened to gospel music she loved that song. To this day, that song still brings tears to my eyes.

My only condolence is that I know where her soul is. There's no guessing or wondering. I know that when it's

my time to go, and I pray to God that I get it together
before then, I will see her in heaven. I truly believe that
every time something bad happens to me, she is my
guardian angel that pulls me right back up and every time
something good happens, it's her that's got my back.

Even though the streets raised me, everything that she
instilled in me is there. I am filled with all the love, the
compassion, and the independence she showed me. She
did whatever it took to get the job done, and had a heart
of gold while doing it. God, I wish my mother was still
here.

I think that I am beginning to understand what a
mother – daughter relationship should be like. I wanna
be like *Tupac's 'Dear Momma'* song. I wish that I could
put money in my mother's mailbox. I feel as though I am
speaking to my mother, through the words of that song. I
would give anything to be able to pick up the phone, and
ask my mother for advice. To just talk to her and let her
know what was going on with me. I wish I could pay
some of her bills, so she wouldn't have to work so hard.

Momma, I am so, so sorry.

There's not a day that goes by that I don't think of my
mother. I walk around everyday with guilt. It's a pain
that I've learned to deal with, that never goes away.

My sister; that's my baby girl. I love her more than I
love myself. I would sacrifice my life so that she could
have hers. She was catching hell in my grandmother's
house. I had a crack-head auntie who lived there. When
she wasn't stealing what she could from the house, she
was raising hell with everybody in the house. In addition
to that, a lot of mess and gossip goes down in that house.
My sister definitely did not get the type of love, or
support, that she got from our mother. We didn't have

the conventional sweet and loving type of grandmother. Don't get me wrong, she loves us, but she had that hard type of love.

I stayed in touch with my sister on a regular basis. If she needed anything, I would send it to her. She received boxes of clothes and shoes all the time. That was nothing. She told me whenever she got a whipping, or if someone was bothering her. Man, I wish I had my own place. My sister needed to be with me. I knew that I had to get my shit together. Not for me, but for her.

CHAPTER 15

Between the streets, my sister, and my friends, there was always something going on in my world. I learned that no matter what cards you are dealt, always play to win. If you are going to do something, do it right the first time. That's why when Asia called me about a money lick, it was a proposition that I couldn't refuse. I was in the middle of a sew-in, trying to finish up.

"Who is that," Star asked when I hung up the phone?

"That was Asia. She'll be here at 6pm to pick me up. She needs my help with something," I replied.

"Are you still going to Lil' Mark's barbecue with us?" La'Mica asked.

"I'm not sure, but I'll let you know," I answered.

"Dog, you're missing out. All of the baller's are going to be in the building. Come on now Destiny," Star said.

"I'll try and meet ya'll there. I'll call and let you know."

I finished my client's hair, and packed a bag. I wanted to be prepared just in case I made it to the party.

It was ten minutes before six o'clock when Asia pulled up in front of the house.

"Damn, that was quick," I said as I got into the car.

"Girl it's going down," Asia said, all hyped up.

"What? What's going down?" I asked.

"Everything is all in motion. All we have to do is be in place, and set it off when it's time to," Asia replied.

We were pulling in her apartment complex. She had a heavy foot, and always pushed it wherever she went.

"Come on, I'll fill you in when we get inside the house."

When I walked in, I saw Alicia and Bernice sitting at the kitchen table.

"What's up Destiny?" Alicia asked.

"Shit. Same thing, different day."

"Now tell me what's going on?" I asked Asia.

"Come in here and sit down. This can never leave this kitchen table," Asia said, looking at all three of us.

After listening to all of the details, I was definitely down. Bernice was hooking up with Mario tonight. They had a room reserved for the weekend. Asia paid a junkie to reserve the adjoining suite over the phone. Mario was waiting for his people to come into town so that he could re-up. This was a major deal. He was purchasing four kilo's of dope, which was equal to $40,000 in cash. He and Bernice had gotten very close, and crept on the regular. He trusted her and wanted her to be his lady. Bernice wasn't no dummy though. She knew that Mario was a whore, and he wasn't going to change. No matter how much money he gave her, she wasn't leaving her baby daddy. Bernice was to leave the door that connected the rooms unlocked. We were to be in our room, waiting for her to call us when he fell asleep. Everything sounded good so far.

Asia went into the bedroom, and returned carrying two duffel bags. One contained four long sleeve, black hooded shirts, four pairs of black pants, and four black ski masks. The other carried four 9 mm pistols in it.

"Whoa, where did you get those?" I asked staring at the guns.

"I got them from my homeboy. They're clean," Asia replied.

"Are we gonna kill him?" Alicia asked.

"This is just for our protection, just in case we need them," Asia answered.

She handed everyone a set of clothes except Bernice.

"Did you get your peoples at Enterprise to hook us up?" Asia asked Alicia.

"Yeah, it's parked outside."

"I got everyone black sneakers and socks," Bernice said grabbing her footlocker bags.

"So let me get this straight. He's never going to know who crept up on him, and we are supposed to walk out of there with all of that money," I asked.

"That's the idea. When we leave, we're gonna take both of their clothes. Sorry Bernice. No one talks. No one says a word," Asia stated.

"I gotta get going. I'm supposed to meet him in a little bit. You guys need to be in the next room before we get there. After I rock his world and put him to sleep, I'll call," Bernice said.

We all walked out the door together and Bernice got into a separate car.

There was no turning back. After this, I was gonna get my life together. With this money, plus what I already had saved, I was gonna be straight. I was ready to do something different. I was tired of running and looking over my shoulders. This was the push that I needed.

It didn't take us long to get to the hotel. We knew that we had beat them there, because we didn't see

Mario's car. We grabbed our bags, and entered through the emergency entrance on the side of the hotel. Once we got into the room, we all changed into the black clothes.

"Here, everyone put on these gloves. No prints can be left in this room. Put all of the clothes that ya'll just took off in this bag," Asia said.

"Shhhh. Do you hear that?" I asked.

"It's them," Alicia replied.

The television was on, and they were talking. We sat in silence, waiting for the phone to ring. The minutes turned into hours. Damn, how long was it going to take for him to go to sleep? The waiting was driving me crazy.

"Listen," I said.

It was Bernice moaning softly. Her moans slowly turned into yells.

"Damn, are they fucking or fighting?" Asia asked.

Alicia and I started laughing.

"Ya'll hoes are so silly," she said trying to hold in her own laugh.

"Yes Daddy. Oh Daddy," Bernice yelled!

Oh my God. I hope this wasn't going to last all night long. Forty-five minutes later, the phone rang.

"He's sleep," Bernice whispered as soon as I answered.

CLICK.

Everyone put on their ski masks, and pulled the hoods over our heads. With our guns in our hands, we quietly went through the adjoining door.

The air conditioner was blasting, and their clothes were scattered all over the floor. Mario was laying flat on his back, and Bernice was curled up beside him. We surrounded the bed, all of our guns were aimed at his face. Bernice opened her eyes and screamed. Mario eyes flew open, and he reached for the nightstand.

"Move and you're dead," I said.

He must have felt the coldness in my voice, because his eyes got wide, and he froze.

"Please don't hurt me," Bernice cried, scooting to the end of the bed.

"If you lay a finger on me, or my girl," Mario said staring me straight in the eyes.

"You'll what! Snitch ass Nigga," Asia yelled!

I walked over to grab the briefcase that was sitting in the corner. My gun was still aimed.

"Make sure that's the money," Asia said.

She didn't have to tell me twice.

"Ya'll bitches better kill me, because ya'll some dead hoes," Mario yelled.

"Oh, that can be arranged," I answered.

At that moment, Asia pulled off her ski mask, and walked over to the bed.

"Remember my aunt Kya and Bee nigga. Remember D-man that you snitched on?" Asia asked.

"Fuck it. Do you remember my man, your first cousin Drake that you snitched on?" I asked.

"Bitch ass nigga! You remember my brother that you killed over a fucking dice game at your party," Alicia yelled!

Boom. One shot to the dome. Blood splattered all over Bernice's face. He was dead, with his eyes wide open.

Bernice jumped out of the bed, and was putting her clothes on. I picked up a clean towel and started wiping the room down. I did not want Bernice's prints anywhere in that room. This was not how we planned that shit.

"I didn't know that was your brother who was killed at his party," Asia said.

"Yeah, he'd just graduated from Pine Forest High School, and was offered a basketball scholarship to college," Alicia answered.

"Let's get out of here," I said after everything had been wiped down.

We went into our room and grabbed our bags. Bernice quickly changed into a set of black clothes. In less than five minutes we were in the car, on the highway, with ten grand apiece in our pockets. Now that's what I'm talking about. I didn't have any remorse. He got what he deserved. I rolled the window down, and let the fresh air hit my face. Everyone was quiet, each of us lost in our own thoughts.

The first thing that we did when we got to the house was split the money. Then we all took turns getting into the shower. I wondered if Star and La'Mica was still at Lil' Mark's party. It was 10:45pm, still kind of early. I dialed Star's number.

"Hello," she answered.

I could hear the loud music in the background.

"How long are you all going to be at the party?" I asked.

"We just got here an hour ago. It's just starting to get live."

"I'll call you when I'm on my way," I replied.

"Alright."

Everyone decided that they wanted to go to the party with me. Bernice left first. Asia and I followed Alicia to the rental car place to drop off the car. She put the keys in the drop box, and left the car parked in front of the building. When we made it there, the party was still crunk. Lil' Mark was the first person that I saw, when we walked in the house.

"What up Destiny? I thought that you weren't going to make it", he said giving me a hug.

"You know that I had to represent for my homeboy."

"What's up Asia? Damn, who's your girl? How you doing Ms. Lady?" he asked directing his attention to Alicia.

"My name is Alicia, and I'm fine," she replied blushing from ear to ear.

"I see that. You ladies make yourselves comfortable. The food and drinks are in the kitchen. Get at me before you leave Alicia," he said as he walked away.

"Girl, who was that," Alicia asked excitedly?

"That's Lil' Mark. He's straight. He's good peoples," I answered.

We walked into the kitchen to fix drinks. I should have known that's where I'd find La'Mica and Star.

"About time," La'Mica said as I walked into the kitchen.

"Whatever lady," I replied happy to see my home girls.

After we made our drinks, we mingled in with the crowd. It was a cool party, and everyone seemed to be enjoying themselves. Where the hell was Bernice? I hadn't seen her yet. I guess she couldn't make it. Everyone was on the dance floor having a good time, while I set back and just watched the crowd. There was some chick the kept eyeballing me. Every time I looked up, the bitch is staring in my face. I've seen her from somewhere before. She was talking to Lil' Mark, and all up in my mouth. I hope that she didn't think that I wanted him, he was just my homeboy. I know where I know this broad from. She was at Mario's party awhile back, when me and Drake was together. This bitch was hating even then. Jocking me and my man like she got some kind of beef. She need to get her some business before I send Alicia over there to holla at Lil' Mark. She would be really pissed off then.

"Asia, do you know that broad who's talking to Lil' Mark," I asked walking on the dance floor?

"Naw, I don't know her, but she be at the R.K.'s every weekend. That's Vani Parks," Asia replied.

"That bitch act like she got some beef. She keeps staring over here like she got a problem. Do we need to set it off up in here," I asked ready to start some shit.

"Naw, chill. She knows what's up. That's why she is over there, and we are over here. She knows better."

"Yeah, I guess," I stated as I walked back over to my chair.

I was not in a good mood, and I was tired. I met a few guys, but I wasn't really interested. I needed to work on me. And I'd be damn if I let another man put his hands on me again.

As the party began to die down, the day's events began to take a toll on me and I was ready to lay it down. I told the crew that I would call them tomorrow and that I was riding home with Star. La'Mica left in her car because she had to be up early for work the next day. I got my bags out of Asia's car, and we all left at the same time.

CHAPTER 16

I laid low the next few weeks, and followed the news closely. Mario had been dead for two days before housekeeping discovered his body. There was a 'Do not Disturb' sign on the door. The police had no evidence, no witnesses, and no suspects. Neither one of us discussed the incident at all, as if nothing ever happened. It's crazy how things happen. Kya's drug charges were dropped, because the state didn't have a witness. She was still sentenced to two years in prison for the interference with custody charge. Her lawyer told her that she wouldn't even serve the whole two years. I was very happy for her.

It was now time for me to get my shit right. I wanted a job, I wanted to go back to school, and I wanted a driver's license. Everybody had a car, and I wanted one too. I was sixteen years old, and my seventeenth birthday was in two weeks. Star and La'Mica both thought that I was already seventeen, going on eighteen.

I knew that they were going to trip out when I told them that they had been hanging out with a sixteen year old, even though they often told me that I acted older than them sometimes. I was the bold one of the group, down for whatever. I was the shit talker that popped off everything when there was a problem. I was always down for a party, even when neither of them was. I was always looking for the after hour spot.

A week had passed and I was still trying to figure out a way to tell them.

"Um, I have something to tell ya'll, something that I've never told ya'll before," I said.

"What is it?" La'Mica asked.

"I don't know how to say it," I answered.

"What is it?" La'Mica asked again impatiently.

"I don't know how to say it."

"Just say it Destiny," Star replied.

"I can't."

I still couldn't fix my mouth to say the words. It had been so long since I spoke my real age, I think that I was kind of confused. No one knew. No one.

The next few days they were guessing all sort of crazy shit.

"Are you pregnant?" La'Mica asked.

"Nope."

"Do you have H.I.V.?" Star asked.

"No!"

"Did you kill somebody?" asked La'Mica.

"No."

"Are you the police?" Star asked.

"Hell No!"

I mean the list got crazier and crazier. Finally, I just came out with it.

"I am only 16yrs old, and I will be seventeen in a few days," I replied.

"What! You mean to tell me that you are the same age as my 'little' sister?" asked Star.

"I don't believe her. This bitch is lying," La'Mica jumped in.

I couldn't help but to laugh.

"For real guys, that's the truth. Now what?" I asked.

After the shock wore off, we all laughed. I was the wildest one, and the youngest one. That day, the three of us formed a bond that would never be broken. We were all sisters. Today, yesterday, and forever.

It was my seventeenth birthday, and Star was getting dressed for work. She had just gotten hired at the cable company, as a customer service rep. I decided, this very day, that I was ready to turn my life around. I wanted to be normal, to live a normal life. I was ready to go back to school.

"Star, can you drop me off at the Juvenile Detention Center on your way to work," I asked?

I should have had a cam-recorder, just to catch the expression on her face.

"You said do what," she asked with an unbelievable look on her face?

I spent so much of my time dodging the police, it was hard to believe that I wanted to go to them.

"I'm ready to get this crap from over my head, and I'm tired of running."

"Happy birthday girl, you are growing up," she replied hugging my neck.

We pulled up in front of the building. She paused before putting the car in park.

"Are you sure," she asked?

"Yeah, I'm sure. I'll holla at you in a minute."

All of my clothes, and possessions were at her house. She would be the first person I saw as soon as I touched down.

When I walked into the intake area, I saw a familiar face. It was one of the counselor's that I saw after I was raped. This was the lady that I would look at and ignore. She looked exactly the same as she did years ago. Her name was Brooke Moseley.

"How can I help you," she asked as I approached her desk?

"My name is Destiny Moore, and there's a warrant out for my arrest. I'm here to turn myself in."

"Destiny Moore, why does that name sound so familiar," she asked?

She had taken a special interest in both of my rape cases years ago. She knew my mother, and all about me. She was determined on counseling me, or helping me, but I had shut her out.

"I remember you. Look at you, you are all grown up now. Where's your mother," she asked?

"She passed away two years ago," I answered.

"Oh, I am so sorry," she said with a look of concern on her face.

I hated when people said that.

We talked, and I filled her in on bits and pieces of my life. She truly was a sweet woman, an extra ordinary woman. I liked her. She got me processed, and ready to go upstairs. She told me that I didn't have to stay, and that I could be released to a guardian until my court date.

"Do you have someone that is willing to be responsible for you? Someone that would meet all of the criteria that the courts would require?" she asked.

I hadn't really thought that far. I only knew that my first step to a new life started right here. Brooke even offered to be my guardian, if she could. I had never met a white woman who was so nice in my life.

I stayed in Juvenile for one week. I still needed a guardian. I hadn't seen Aunt Donna in a while, and had no idea how to get in touch with her. I couldn't think of anyone else. My two options are go to my grandmother's house in Mississippi or stay in a group home until I became emancipated.

I was choosing option #2. I was 17yrs old, and Theresa said that she didn't think that the judge would have a problem granting my request, given my situation. She was willing to go to court and stand up for me, if she had to.

Out of the blue, in the middle of the night, the correction officer yelled, 'Pack it up!' What the hell was this all about? I don't think they are sending me to a group home at this time of the night.

After I was dressed back into my own clothes, I was taken to the waiting area of the intake department. I sat there for about ten minutes. Then I saw her walk out. It was Star's mom, Mrs. Elaine.

"Hey baby," she said giving me a hug.

I was shocked. I didn't know what to think, or expect. Everything was happening so fast. Within thirty minutes, we were on our way to Mrs. Elaine's house. My new home.

I already knew everybody in the house, so it wasn't like I was a stranger. It was Mrs. Elaine, her husband, and their two daughters. The oldest was Rita, she was 19 and had her own room. The younger sister, Princess, and I were the same age and we shared a room.

I had been in this same house, with these same people, drinking cocktails and chilling with moms and pops. I had even stood outside on the carport with Star smoking a blunt. This was a totally different ball game though, the rules and positions had changed. I could deal with that. That is what this was all about right, change?

My next few days were hectic. Mrs. Elaine and I were everywhere. We went from office to office. She was basically starting from scratch. We needed my school transcripts from my previous school, my birth certificate, my social security card, and a death certificate for my mother. She needed all of these things in order to enroll me in school.

Social security had never been filed for my mom, I never applied for it. It was now being applied for. As my guardian, Mrs. Elaine was given back pay from two years ago when my mother first passed away. It was over $8,000. Plus, she received $450 monthly. I saw little to none of that back pay check. She opened a checking account in my name, but she was the primary account holder. It literally was for show, because I never had access to it.

She bought brand new tires for her van, and things for her house. She took me school shopping for clothes, and I wanted to scream. Every store that she went to, I would have never gone to. I was so pissed off! I am trying to stay respectful, because this was Star's mom, but this is what takes the cake! When she got the first monthly check, she told me that all I needed was $50 monthly to buy all of my personal hygiene products like my soap, toothpaste, toothbrush, douche, tampons, and the rest. I could have hit the floor!

First of all, this money is not money that the state is giving her to take care of me. This is money that my mother has worked hard for all her life. It's that small tax that they take from each and every one of your paychecks, called social security. This lady has lost her mind. She didn't even want me to work a part-time job. She was too afraid that if I made too much that they would cut the social security check.

Oh, hell no! I wasn't taking this shit anymore. I could have stayed in a group home and became emancipated. At least that way, I could have had my own money. I wasn't broke by far, but that was none of her business.

The following day while at school, I called Brooke Moseley from the detention center. I told her everything that had been going on. She sounded more upset than I was.

"I'd rather stay in a group home than in this woman's house," I told her.

"When school let's out, don't get on the bus. I'll be there to pick you up," she said and hung up the phone.

Just like she promised, she was outside of the Jr. College waiting. I had dropped out of school in the 9th grade. Instead of going back to a regular high school, I went to a Jr. College that offered a high school diploma program. I didn't want a G.E.D. I still needed the same amount of credits in the same subjects. There were adults and Teenagers in my classes. It was just like college. The teachers would give out assignments and expect you to turn them in on time. If not, you got a zero. No one was riding your back to make sure that you did your work. I enjoyed being in class. I liked the challenge.

I spotted her standing by her car in front of the building. I walked over to her with my books in my hand.

"Hey Turkey," she said.

She always called me that. I started laughing.

"Hi, Mrs. Moseley."

"What did I tell you? Call me Brooke," she said

teasingly.

We got in the car and headed to Mrs. Elaine's house.

"I've already filed the proper paperwork to have you removed from the home, but you have to go in front of the judge and tell him what's going on," she said.

"I don't know if I can," I said nervously.

"Just tell him everything that you told me, and you'll be fine."

I saw Mrs. Elaine's van parked in the yard, as we pulled in front of the house.

"Go and get your things, and I will do the talking," she said.

I don't know what they talked about, and I didn't care. I packed my bags, and returned to the car.

So here I am, back in the Juvenile detention center. It's all good though. I just didn't want Star and I to fall out about her mother. I had been telling her what was going on. She really didn't want to get involved. She chose to stay out of it. I don't blame her, I probably would have too. I mean, she can't control what her mother does and at the end of the day, that's still her mother. On the other hand, I think that she felt where I was coming from as well. It was an ugly situation all the way around.

During the whole ordeal, I confided in this chick that braided my hair. Her name was Wanda. We didn't hang out or anything, she was someone that I could talk to. She was very good peoples, and she could braid the hell out of some hair. She couldn't believe that Star's mom had done all of that. I called her from the detention center to tell her where I was at.

One whole day had passed since I had been in this camp. It was eight o'clock in the morning when I heard,

"Moore, pack it up."

Here we go again. They must have found a spot for me at one of the group homes. Once again, I am dressed and back into my own clothes. I am taken to the waiting area, and waiting in intake. After sitting there for about thirty minutes, a woman walks into the lobby area.

"Who is this lady," I wondered to myself?

Brooke walked into the lobby behind her. The unknown woman walked over to me with an extended hand.

"Hello. My name is Ms. Lox, and I am Wanda's mom," she said.

I didn't know what to say. The tears just rolled down my face. She then hugged my neck and held me tight.

I could not believe the compassion of this beautiful woman. She didn't know me from a can of paint, yet she willing to take me into her home. It felt like she had been sent from an angel. Like my mother had sent her. This felt right.

We made small talk on the way to her house. I found out that she works for H.R.S. (The Department of Health and Rehabilitation Services). That's pretty much everything from welfare, to food stamps, to child protective services. She had a seventeen year old daughter named Makeba, and a twelve year old daughter name Courtney. They both lived in the house.

When we arrived at her house, I was instantly impressed. She lived in a brand new home, in a new subdivision. It was a four bedroom house, with two and a half baths, and a library with books from wall to wall. There was a pool in the back yard, and a screened in porch.

I loved it there, it was peaceful. I had my own room,

and got along well with both of her daughters. Makeba drove her own car, and would take me to school everyday. They had an older sister, Tony, who was off in college. She came home on a regular basis. We got along well also. Ms. Lox was cool as hell, but she did not play the radio. As long as you did what you were supposed to do, then everything was good.

My life was starting to fall into place. I got a job at the movie theatre working at night, and went to school during the day. I was taking Driver's Education on Saturday's, as one of my electives, so that I could get my driver's license. Plus, I still had homework to do. Church was optional on Sunday mornings, but everyone else went so I went too. I was enjoying my new life.

Once I was settled into my new home and used to my everyday routine, I had Makeba take me to Star's place. I still had lots of brand name clothes and shoes over there. More importantly, that's where I had my money stashed. I never told her about it, and I was praying that it was still there.

"Give me a minute," I told Makeba as I got out of the car.

"No problem," she stated.

Before I got a chance to knock, Star opened the door.

"Hey Destiny," she said with a Kool-Aid smile on her face.

"Hey Ms. Lady. What's been going on?" I asked.

"Nothing much, just working hard."

We walked into the house and sat down. I briefly told her how my life was going, and let her know that everything was all good.

"You are still my sister," she said.

"I love you, and you will always be my sister," I

117

answered.

I went into my old room and got all of my belongings. The very first thing that I checked for was my money. Thank God, it was all there. Everything was all good. I began to pack all of my things. Star helped me to load it all in the car.

"You better keep in touch. Tell La'Mica to call me," I told her as I got in the car.

"I will, love you," she yelled.

"I love you too!"

The school year was over in May, but I still didn't stop. I went the school the entire summer semester. I was trying to get all of my credits, and still graduate with my correct class. My class graduated that May, if I pushed myself, then I would graduate in December. That means that I would stay in school all summer, and the first half of the regular school year. No breaks.

Brooke and Ms. Lox stayed in touch. Brooke also remained a permanent figure in my life. I constantly talked to my sister Gia in Mississippi. She even came down to visit me at Ms. Jamie's place, and stayed a couple of weeks during the summer. My life was actually on track now. I opened a checking account and had my pay checks directly deposited. Working, along with the money I had saved, left me more than okay.

My eighteenth birthday was two weeks away, and I couldn't wait. I spoke with Ms. Lox and told her that I wanted to look for an apartment, and move into my own place. She was very supportive. I also shared with her that I wanted to get custody of my little sister. I wanted her to live with me. She told me to let her know when I was ready, and she would show me exactly what I needed to do.

LITTLE LOST GIRL

I found a nice two bedroom apartment in Lincoln Park. It was close to my job, and not far from my school. I paid the rent, deposit, and connected the utilities. I moved in on my eighteenth birthday. At last, I had my own shit!

Wanda gave me one of her old bedroom sets, until I had a chance to buy new furniture. It didn't matter to me, I was just happy to be in my own place. Everyone came by to bring me house warming gifts. I didn't have to buy much. The very first night La'Mica and Star came over, and we smoked out. They brought everything for the kitchen and bathroom. Asia brought over a new comforter set, and Alicia had a big ass bottle of Remy Martin. Tammy had given me a living room set that she had in storage. I was happy that all of my friends had come through to show some love.

Monday morning, it was business as usual. It was school during the day, and work at night. I was now receiving my own social security checks, because I was still a student, and began looking for a car. I needed my own mode of transportation bad. I was tired of bumming rides, and catching buses. I need the right car for the right price. My biggest problem was time. If I wasn't in school, I was always at work and things weren't slowing down. I was too close to graduation and I had to get every dollar that I can.

CHAPTER 17

One weekend I agreed to go on a double date with Star, her new boyfriend, and his brother. I had been working so hard and finally had a weekend off. I needed a break. All I really wanted to do was sit down at the house and chill, but she insisted that I get out of the house.

"Girl put some clothes on, I'm coming to get you," she said persistently over the phone.

"This is my first weekend off in awhile and I just want to relax," I told her trying to get out of it.

"I promise you're going to have fun. When was the last time that you've went anywhere," she asked?

"I don't know, where are you guys going?" I asked still undecided.

"We're trying to figure that out. The state fair is here, maybe we'll check that out. Just put some clothes on, we'll be there in an hour."

"Damn. I'll get dressed, but I'm not staying out too late. His brother better not be ugly or I'm gonna kick your ass," I replied jokingly.

"I promise you won't regret it. See you in a minute," she said laughing before hanging up the phone.

They pulled up in front of my apartment in exactly an hour. Star introduced me to her new boyfriend and his brother. His brother's name was Deon, and that nigga was tight to death. I mean from head to toe. The nigga was definitely a baller and he was cute as hell! The best part about him though, was that he was cool as shit. We were digging each other all night long. We went to the state fair and had a ball. We took pictures, played games, and rode the scariest roller coaster rides. I really enjoyed myself. Our chemistry was as if we already knew each other. It was crazy. We acted like big kids. By the end of the night I had all kinds of stuffed animals. I don't ever remember having this much fun with anyone on a date. We talked about everything from music, to movies, to politics, and the bible. At the end of the night we exchanged numbers and agreed to keep in touch.

After that night, Deon started coming by the house all the time. I no longer had to catch rides, or busses. We had lots of long, serious talks and I shared things with him about me, my past, and my mother. Things that I had never confided in anyone about before, I shared with Deon and he had become my best friend. Within a couple of months, we were officially an item.

It was a Thursday afternoon, and I was just walking out of my last class. Just like clockwork, Deon was pulling up in front of the school.

"How was school?" he asked as I got in the car.

"It was cool. I can't wait until I graduate though."

"You are almost there baby girl," he said as he reached over and gave me a kiss on my forehead before we pulled off.

He was so positive. He made me feel like the sky is the limit. I know that I can do anything that I put my mind to, but to have that support system and someone encouraging me, was something that I was lacking. He pushed me about things in a way that a mother, or father would. I had become dependent on his thoughts and opinions.

"Where are we going?" I asked.

"Just ride, you'll see."

Deon was very spontaneous. You never knew what to expect with him. Everybody loved him because he was good peoples. You couldn't help but to love him because his sincerity showed. We went to a drive-through to get something to eat. I wasn't really that hungry, so I ordered a chicken salad. I had just eaten on my lunch break and so I wasn't that hungry. We pulled up in front of a furniture store and he parked.

"Why are we here?" I asked.

"You need a living room set, a new one. Plus, you need to get rid of that waterbed, it makes my back hurt," he said smiling while rubbing his neck.

I didn't know what to say, I was speechless. At that moment I knew that he was the right one for me.

We walked around the entire store until we found the right color, comfort, and style for me. In addition to the living room and bedroom set, we got a second bedroom set for the empty room, and an elegant dining room table with four large chairs to match. I knew that my sister would be here soon, and I wanted everything to be ready for her. Deon looked for a big screen television for the living room, while I picked out a couple of huge wall paintings and mirrors to match the furniture. He paid for everything in cash, and it was scheduled to be delivered in a couple of hours.

Once we left there, we went to Wal-mart and purchased everything else we needed for the house. Last, we went to the grocery store so that we could pack the refrigerator and freezer. When we finally made it home, the furniture truck was pulled up a few minutes later. Deon paid the delivery guys extra to put the old furniture out. After the new furniture was all set up, the place looked totally different. I was amazed.

"Thank you so much Deon. You didn't have to do all of this," I said happily.

"No problem. I just want to be comfortable whenever I'm in town," he replied.

"What am I going to do with this old furniture," I asked looking out of the front door?

"Don't worry about it. I'll have my peoples to pick it up, and put it back into storage."

I hugged him and gave him a long, passionate kiss. This was my baby.

From that moment on, we were inseparable. We would go to the bookstore together, at least twice a week. That was one of my favorite things. It was very relaxing to sit in the café area, sip on cappuccino, and read a good book. I also found a lot of interesting literature that related to some of my classes. History was one of my favorite subjects, especially African-American history. I never knew that the Blackman performed the first open heart surgery, invented the washing machine, and invented the first traffic light. All of those things excited me. I was like a kid in a candy store. Deon liked to do his bible study. He would have different religious books, taking notes from each one of them. When there was something that he didn't understand, we would figure it out together. We became very close. He was totally different from any guy that I'd ever met. He never pushed himself on me. We started out as really good friends.

In the meantime, Ms. Lox and I were working on the legal paperwork to obtain custody of my seventeen year old sister. It wasn't really that hard, because my grandmother didn't contest anything. Within one month, my sister was on the greyhound bus, and on her way to Florida. Deon and I were at the bus stop anxiously waiting for her. Thank you Jesus! I had my little sister back. As soon as she walked off the bus, and into the bus station, I ran over to her and hugged her neck. I had part of my family back. Little did I know we were expecting a new member to the family.

Gia's room was totally hooked up. She had a new five piece bedroom set, a cable ready television set, and a stereo system. It was also complete with a full wardrobe with new tags hanging in the closet. Her dresser drawers were full with new undergarments and Tee-shirts. Personal hygiene and hair products were sitting on the dresser. She had everything that she needed. If she needed anything, all she had to do was ask.

I opened a checking account in her name, and had her social security checks directly deposited into her account. I also enrolled her to the same Jr. College for the next semester. She was two months pregnant, and you couldn't even tell it. The second day that she was there she broke the news to me. She was excited about it. I think that she wanted someone to love, to take the place of the love that was missing from our mother. We set her up with Medicaid and WIC, and she was assigned her own doctor. My sister and the baby were both healthy. I was going to be an Auntie! I couldn't wait. This baby was going to be spoiled rotten.

The months were passing by, and I was getting closer to graduation. Deon ordered my cap, gown, and class ring. I can't believe that I was actually about to graduate. Just a year ago, I was running the streets without a care in the world. No goals, no life. No expectations for the future. I had transformed into a responsible, mature, beautiful young lady.

Ms. Lox, Deon, Star, La'Mica, Gia, Brooke, Wanda, Asia, Bernice, and Alicia were all there. I felt so proud to walk across that stage. When they called my name, my family and friends all yelled my name too. I graduated with honors, having maintained a 3.5 GPA and I received another special certificate to commemorate it. The ceremony was beautiful. I couldn't have asked for a better day. All of the blood, sweat, and tears were worth this one moment. I wish that my mother could have been here. Even though she wasn't present in body, I knew that she was here in spirit. I did all of this for her. I wanted to show her that even though I was a rebellious child, she did a wonderful job as a mother. I wanted to thank her for the countless times that she prayed for me. Because of those prayers, I am still here today.

And guess what, I'm not finished yet. I planned on going to college, and getting some type of degree. I just wasn't sure what yet. I didn't want to work hard all of my life just to make ends meet. I didn't want to depend on a man for my livelihood. I enrolled at the same Jr. College for a two year degree. The plan was to stay there for two years, then transfer to a university. In the meantime, I continued to work, go to class, and spend time with my sister.

Deon was a big help. He took care of everything in the house, and bought me a car as my graduation gift. My very first car was a big body Mercedes Benz 3420. It was black with peanut butter seats. Deon knows how much I love music, so he had a stereo system installed, and put knock in the trunk. My car was almost identical to his, except his car was money green, with gold specs in the paint. I think that he kind of bought it for himself too, so that we could switch up. Deon had a friend that worked at the auction so there were no car notes. The insurance policies were paid up for a whole year, so all I had to do was keep gas in it, keep the maintenance up, and drive. While I went to school and worked, if my sister needed anything at any time she called Deon. He loved my sister just as much as I did, and she was crazy about her brother-in-law.

One day after school, I was headed to work, I received a phone call from Deon.

"Hello," I answered.

"Destiny, can you see if you can take off of work this weekend? I would like for us to take a trip."

"Where do you want to go? I'll try. Normally, we have to submit the request two weeks in advance," I answered excitedly.

"Alright, see what you can do, and let me know," he answered.

"Okay baby. I love you."

"I love you too baby."

We made it a point never to hang up the phone without saying those three words.

I gave my shift to a girl that need some extra hours. Everything was approved through management, so I was cool. I really didn't have to work, but I would feel crazy if every penny that I had came from a man. There was a nice balance in my account, but if I never added to it, then it would decrease. That was something that I couldn't let happen. Plus, I enjoyed being around and interacting with people. I worked in the mall, so I was in everybody's business. I knew who was with who, and who was cheating on who. This was sort of a release after being in class all day long.

It was a typical Tuesday at work, and we were extremely slow that night. Everyone stood around talking and laughing. Customers were walking through the door, so we all took our positions at our registers. You would have thought I saw Tupac walk through the doors. I froze, in shock. I couldn't move. I had to be seeing things. How could this be? He was locked up!! He was with a girl that I had seen somewhere before. It was the chick that was all in my grill when we went to Mario's party a long time ago.

"Destiny, is that you," Drake asked as he walked up to my counter?

"How long have you been out? I thought that you were still locked up," I asked trying to maintain my balance?

"I've been home for a month. I heard that you were doing well, but I didn't know how to find you," he answered.

I was speechless. I didn't know what to do or say.

"You are all grown up now," he said.

Drake still looked the same, just a little heavier and he still looked good. All of a sudden, I began to feel dizzy.

"Can you give me a minute? I'll meet you down in the food court," he asked the chick that he was with.

She walked away, but not before giving me a dirty look.

We sat down and talked. I told him my mother had passed away, and that I had went back to school and graduated.

"Are you okay?" he asked.

"Yeah, I'm okay."

"I've heard. They say that you're with the big weight man, and that you're living good. I understand if you've moved on. I know that you had to do what you had to do."

I was fighting hard to hold back my tears.

"Desi, I will always love you. If you need anything, let me know."

I would always love Drake. He would always have a special place in my heart.

"Can I see you sometimes?" he asked.

"Drake, you know that would not be a good idea. Please, don't do this," I pleaded.

"Those whole four and a half years, all I've thought about is you. Can I at least get a hug?"

As I hugged his neck, the tears that I fought to hold, were now falling. We held each other for a few moments before I pulled away. Damn, why did it have to happen like this? I took his number, stuck it in my pocket, and went back to work. I didn't notice that the chick that he walked in with across the hall, in the bookstore, glaring at us.

CHAPTER 18

It was the weekend already. Gia and I were preparing for our trip to New Orleans. Deon wanted to shop, and got a gold grill. I had scheduled the appointment for the three of us with the dentist there. Gia wanted two gold teeth, I was dropping five, and Deon already had six on the bottom, and was dropping another six at the top.

We had a ball in New Orleans. We walked down Bourbon Street drinking Hurricanes and shopping. We shopped at all of the malls, and ate Cajun food the entire weekend. My baby looked good with his new twelve-pack. I was feeling my grill as well. My sister looked jazzy with her two-pack. We came home all blinged up, and with plenty of bags. I had already started shopping for the baby. She had so many diapers, onesies, bottles, and pampers. We bought so many baby girl outfits it was pathetic. I could not wait until she got here.

The months rolled by, and Gia's stomach was getting bigger, and bigger. La'Mica and I planned a huge baby shower at club house in the apartment complex. We prepared all of the food and refreshments. The barbecue grill was still smoking on the patio. All types of foods were displayed on the table, and there was spiked and non-spiked punch available. Of course, there was a full bar too for those who wanted a real drink. It was a baby shower/party. I invited all of my girl friends. We played games and gave away prizes. Everyone had a good time. Gia had everything that she needed and more. I couldn't wait for my niece to get here. I was going to be an Auntie!

August 14th was the day that my sister bore a beautiful baby girl. She named her Neveah. I had never felt anything like this before. I felt like I was the father. Instantly, I fell in love with my niece. Deon was crazy about her too. He loved kids. They stayed in the hospital for three days before they were released and I waited on Gia and Neveah hand and foot. I had even taken two weeks off from work. While I went to school, Deon was there. My Niece was beautiful. We took all kinds of pictures all the time. We didn't have many baby pictures of ourselves, so we made sure that Neveah had lots.

My niece was now almost three months, and you know who shows up at the door. Yep, it was the baby daddy. Now, all of a sudden, he wants to do right by his child. Now he loves my sister, and wants his family to come home with him, all the way in Mobile, Alabama. OH HELL NO!! I wasn't feeling this. "I" was her family. They belonged here with me. There was a big confrontation between him and me. Gia heard the commotion at the door, and came to the front of the house.

"What's going on Destiny?" she asked walking to the door.

When she saw him standing there, she seemed very shocked. She never really talked about him much, so I didn't know what to think of it.

"Destiny, can you give us a minute please?" Gia asked.

"Okay, but I'll be in the back if you need me," I replied.

I went into my room and called Deon. I was getting upset as I explained to him what was going on.

"Baby, you need to calm down. They are a family. Your sister is not a child, she is a woman now. You have to let her go and find her own way," Deon said calmly.

"But what about my niece?" I asked.

"We can have our own children, and you can see Neveah as much as you like, okay," he said.

"Okay, I guess you are right. I will call you back. I have to check on my sister."

"I'll see you later. Love you."

"I love you too," I answered.

Gia decided to try and make it work. She said that she still loved him and wanted them to be a family. My sister is a very private person, so I never really know how she feels, or what's going on in her mind. He wanted to marry my sister, so that his wife and daughter would have his last name. So there it was. There was no changing her mind. They were married the following week at the courthouse in Mobile, Al. My sister and I talked constantly and we agreed that we would visit each other all the time. I wanted to make sure that my niece knew her auntie.

CHAPTER 19

While I was dealing with all of this, Drake was across town, trying to get his weight up. He picked right up where he left off at. It was as if he never went anywhere. Drake started setting up shop on different blocks. He pulled out guns on people, running them away from their own hoods. Drake had the Westside on lock. With Mario out of the picture, there was no competition. Word on the street was that Mario had snitched on, and set up a lot of people. The rumor around town was that the Miami niggas had murdered him execution style. Drake moved up in rank very fast.

He had a plan in mind. He figured if he had more paper than Deon, and maybe found some dirt on him, that he would get his girl back. Drake did not like Deon, and couldn't wait to catch him slipping on the streets. That was not going to happen. Deon did not club, or hang in the streets. He was a business and family man, period. He loved nice things, but he didn't flaunt it.

Drake had been asking questions about me and Deon around town. He knew the hours that I went to school and work. It was harder for him to figure out Deon's schedule though, because you never knew when he was in town.

There were plenty of females that he dealt with, but

he didn't have a main girl. He was waiting on Desi. He bought a brand new whip, and stayed iced up. Females were always in his face, and nigga's always hated. Clubbing, and popping bottles was his thing. I guess he was trying to make up for the time that he missed. Drake even bought a condo on the beach. I heard this was a straight up bachelor's pad.

He was knocking off this broad that I had a class with. Her name is Iesha. Everyone knew that I was his girl before he got locked up, and that he wanted to get back with me. They also knew who Deon was, and that we were a couple. Iesha came to class one day and made it a point to let me know that she was with Drake last night, and that he was picking her up from school. As if I gave a damn. These broads were so petty. It was funny to me. I couldn't believe that they thought they were special because they were sleeping with nigga's who had money. They didn't have no claims to the money, and the only thing that they got was a wet ass. These were some dumb hoes. These broads need to get their own paper, and then they can holler at me.

The bell had just rang, and that was my last class of the day. I put my books in my backpack, and walked to my car. Damn, this nigga got nerve! He was sitting on the trunk of my car.

"Get the hell off my car," I yelled!

"Oh, that's how you talk to me now," he asked all laid back?

"What the hell do you want Drake? Aren't you supposed to be picking up Iesha?"

"That trick, I just wanted to see you."

"That's messed up Drake. Go and find that girl and take her home," I replied.

"She knows what my car looks like. Look, she's getting in it now," he stated pointing at his car.

I just shook my head. She was pissed off. It was written all over her face.

"Where is your nigga at," he asked?

"Minding his business," I replied starting to get irritated.

"I ain't no hater or nothing, but I care about you Desi. Am I wrong for not wanting to see you get hurt?"

"Yo, what the hell are you talking about," I cut in?

"He's knocking off light skinned Egypt, from the Westside. They say that he's caking her too, but she ain't driving no Benz though," he said while checking out my car.

Pissed off was an understatement. No, no, this was not true. Not 'my' Deon. We talked about everything. This was my best friend Drake was talking about.

"You don't have to believe me, check it out for yourself," he said as if he were reading my thoughts.

"You got the number, give me a call when you find out."

He blew me a kiss and walked away.

My thoughts were racing everywhere. I sat in my car for at least five minutes before I even put the keys in the ignition. My nerves were so bad that I couldn't stop my legs from shaking. I had to calm down. Deon was supposed to be in Miami for the past three days. I just spoke with him this morning before school. I just know he wasn't trying me. Did he not know that I knew people everywhere?

I didn't want to talk on the phone and drive while I was upset, so I waited until I got home. I knew exactly who I was gonna call. She knew everybody on the

Westside. Plus, it had been a minute since I heard from her.

"Hello," Bernice answered.

"What's up girl, this is Destiny."

"Nothing much over here, just slow motion. What's good," she asked?

"I don't know if you can help me, but I need some information."

"What's up," she asked ready to update me on whatever gossip.

"Do you know a light skinned chick name Egypt? They say she lives on the Westside."

"Girl please, who in the hell doesn't know Egypt? She lives on the same street as Bang, right around the corner," Bernice replied.

"What do you know about her," I asked?

"She's had every dope boy in the hood, and that bitch is always keeping shit up. What's going on," she asked?

I hesitated for a moment. It hurt me to even think about it.

"I'm trying to find out if my man is cheating on me. Have you ever seen a green Mercedes Benz over there," I asked?

"Sometimes, but not a lot. It's over there now. I just picked my daughter up from Bang's and it was in the driveway."

Steam was blowing out of my ears.

"Bernice, thank you. I'll call you back later," I said angrily, hanging up the phone.

I couldn't believe that nigga had me fooled! I didn't see this coming. I walked over to the stereo and popped in *Mary J. Blige's* cd. I turned it to one of my favorite tracks *'Not Gonna Cry'*. Every note she sang, the stronger I felt. Listening to Mary was like food to the soul. I picked up the phone, and dialed Deon's number.

"Hey baby. What's up," he answered on the first ring.

"You know what Deon, I thought that you were different," I fumed, my voice full of anger and disappointment.

"What are you talking about? I'll be home tomorrow."

"You know what, you can stay at that bitch Egypt's house. Come and get your shit from over here," I yelled!

"Baby, baby, it's not what you think! I am on my way home," he yelled!

I hung up. I didn't want to hear anymore lies.

Deon never made it to my house. He was pulled over on his way. I found out later that he was sleeping with Egypt, and he had also set up shop at her house. He used her spot to cook up dope that he was bringing in from the bottom. That still didn't mean that he had to sleep with her. After our conversation, Deon had gathered his things, took the work that he had left, and headed to my house. When he was pulled over, the officers searched the car. He was charged with possession of crack cocaine, with intent to distribute. His brother hired the best attorney in town. The possession charge was thrown out, for illegal search. There was no probable cause to search the vehicle. Deon was blessed!! He only had to serve six months for the violation of probation. He called me almost every single day with an apology.

I started conversing with Drake again, while Deon was locked up. I didn't feel like I was doing anything wrong, plus I had no intentions on sleeping with Drake. I told Deon all of this. I wasn't going to be a liar like he was. I honestly didn't know what I wanted to do when Deon came home. Drake was the perfect gentleman. I knew that he still loved me, and I still loved him too. I just wasn't sure if I was still in love with him. Things were so different now, and a lot had happened in my life. It felt good being around him again, but it just didn't seem right.

On my off days we would meet up and catch a movie, or have dinner. I was lonely, upset, and confused. I would not let Drake come to my house, even though he knew where I stayed. It was like I had to get used to him all over again.

We went to visit his mom. He told me that she had been diagnosed with lung cancer, and she wasn't doing too good. When she saw me, she remembered exactly who I was. Her eyes were misty, as she weakly gave me a hug. She had lost a lot of weight and my heart went out to her.

Drake and I had long talks, there was so much to catch up on. He couldn't believe all of the things that I'd gone through.

"I'm sorry for not being there to take care of you," Drake said, eyes full of compassion.

"It's not your fault," I replied

"Do you know that you are the only reason that I made it through prison," he asked?

God, I missed him. He was the same person that I fell in love with. I thought that I would never see him again, and here he was.

He wanted me to move into his place with him, and for me to be his lady again. He told me that the only reason that he'd been running the streets was because I wasn't with him. He promised me that he would come home every night. I was so confused. I mean, Deon had been my best friend and lover. He was there for me through a lot. But still, he had lied to me and cheated on me. Drake had never lied, or cheated. Isn't this what I've been waiting for? Haven't I Dreamed of this day? So why in the hell was I hesitating?

"Just think about it and let me know. Okay Desi?" he asked.

I nodded my head yes.

It was getting late and I had to get home. I had classes early in the morning. Before I could get off the couch, he pulled me into his arms, and kissed me. His kiss was so full of passion, that I was lost. I clung tighter to him. I didn't want to let go. I wanted him. I needed him. No, no, what was I thinking? This was wrong, but it felt so right! I had to stop. If I didn't do it now, then I wouldn't.

"Drake, no. Not yet," I said breathing heavily. "I need a little more time."

"I don't know why you are holding back. I know that you still love a nigga, but I understand. Just a little more time," he replied.

He walked me to my car and I left. I'm going to pray long and hard about this, before going to bed. God work it out.

Three months had passed since Deon had gotten locked up, and I was no closer to a decision. Even though Drake wasn't letting go, I could tell that he was getting frustrated. We still have not had sex yet, and this was becoming a problem. I could see the lust in his eyes every time we were around each other. I could feel the tension starting to build between us. After all, what could I expect, he was a man. I didn't blame him.

Deep down inside, I felt like this belonged to Deon, and I didn't want to give it up to anyone else, even though he did cheat on me. Is that crazy or what?? I received my confirmation when I wouldn't accept money from Drake. He tried to give me money for the rent, and anything else that I had to take care of. I told him that I was good. That was the unspoken moment of truth for the both of us.

The big difference, I think, between Deon and Drake was that Deon was older, more mature, and settled. He was wiser, and he taught me lots of things about life. Drake was only four years older than me, and still had a lot of wild ways. That's what I based my decision on. I know that I hurt him, but I felt like I was making the best decision for me.

I started hearing less of Drake. He didn't call or come around as much. I kept in touch with his mom though. I went by every other day or so to check on her. I wanted to make sure that she didn't need anything. On the days that I didn't go over, I would call. She was a very sweet lady, and I knew that she wouldn't be around too long. This was eating at Drake. He was very close to his mom. I could definitely relate.

I had taken the following week off from work. I was working on a huge project for my biology class, and the report was due next week. Drake's mom called and asked me if I could come over to help her with some laundry, and I agreed. If there was anything that I could help her with, I was more than happy to do it.

I packed a bag for a couple of days since I didn't have to work. I also brought all of my research material with me so that I could work on my project. I cooked, cleaned, and washed clothes. We were talking and laughing about old times and she seemed less stressed; less worried the more that she laughed. I was glad that I was there to keep her company. In some strange sort of way, I felt like I was kind of making up for not doing these things for my mother.

Drake came in and out at least twice a day. Each time he spoke to both of us, and kissed us both on the cheeks. I slept in his old room while I was there. It had been so long since I was in that room, yet everything still looked exactly the same. The second night that I was there, in the wee hours of the morning, I was awakened by the sound of rattling keys, and heavy footsteps walking in the front door. What in the hell was he doing here at this time of the morning? Why didn't he go home, where he lived? I could hear his footsteps coming down the hallway. My heart was racing, I was wide awake. He walked into the room, and stripped down to his boxers. Damn, why did he have to smell so good?? I laid there in total silence staring at his magnificent body. He closed and locked the bedroom door, and then made his way to the bed in the dark. He wrapped his arms around me, and held me tightly. God this felt so good. The touch of his skin against mine set my whole body on fire. Drake had stripped off my t-shirt and panties, then started kissing my breast, my stomach, and then went lower to my clit. This was driving me crazy. His fingers were rubbing my nipples at the same time. I was having orgasm after orgasm, they just wouldn't stop.

"Drake, please baby, put it in," I begged.

But he wouldn't stop. I was pulling the sheets off the bed, trying not to scream. He got up, reached in his jeans pocket, and grabbed a condom. We made love all night long.

"Desi, will you be my wife, and have my babies," he asked?

"Yes baby," I answered, in the moment of passion.

I was gone, carried away by the waves of ecstasy.

I was rudely awakened by the buzzer of the alarm clock. It was 7:45, and my first class starts at 9:00 am. I turned the alarm clock off, got up, and took a shower. I was dressed, and ready to go in forty-five minutes. I gave Drake a kiss on the cheek, after staring at his handsome face. If only I didn't have class today…. Damn, I had to go.

Did last night just happen, or was it all a Dream!!!???? I still had an afterglow on my face. I smiled all day in school. Throughout the day I received several text messages from Drake. They all read, "I love you Desi." I loved him too!!

After school, I went home instead of Drake's mother house. I had to get my thoughts together. They were all together before last night. I needed someone to talk to so I called Gia. She could help me sort everything out.

The next few weeks, I threw myself into school, refusing all of Deon's calls. I also refused to see Drake. I needed some me time. Deon was coming home next month, and Drake was still persistent. My girl Bernice kept me posted on what was going on in the hood, and what Drake was up to. She told me that Drake was caking some chick, but she didn't know her name. She felt like I was crazy for pushing Drake away, and wanted to see the two of us together again.

"If only you knew Deon, you wouldn't feel that way," I told her.

"Maybe so, but I know Drake, and I know that he really loves you," Bernice said, as she began to cry.

"What's wrong? Why are you crying?" I asked.

"I'm alright. I don't want to talk about it right now," she replied.

"Do you need for me to come over?" I asked.

"No, it's okay. I'm cool."

"Just say the words. You know that I will be there."

"How about I come by your place tomorrow evening? I have some clothes that you may want to buy," Bernice replied.

"That'll work. Maybe we can go somewhere and have a few drinks. It sounds like the both of us need to get out," I replied.'

"Alright, cool. I'll be there."

The next evening, Bernice pulled up in my driveway in Lil' Bean's truck. Now this ride was tight. He drove a brand new black Lincoln Navigator, a chrome front grille, chrome trimmings, 24-inch rims, and it had four flat screen televisions in it. We were riding in the Navigator tonight!!!

Bernice came in carrying all types of bags. She had everything from clothes, purses, shoes, accessories, and all. She brought the mall to you. Everything she had fit perfectly, and was exactly my size. I poured both of us a glass of Remy Martin on the rocks while we talked and got dressed.

"Why were you so upset yesterday?" I asked, while rolling up a blunt.

"Things have just been so crazy for me lately, and I have a lot on my mind," Bernice answered.

"Well what's going on?"

"This is only between me and you. This CANNOT leave this room," she said.

"You know better than that. How long have you known me?" I asked.

"Yeah, I know. I have been holding this in for months, and I really need a friend to talk to," she replied, with tears already forming in the corners of her eyes.

I placed my glass on the dresser, and sat on the bed next to her, giving her my full attention.

"Take your time. Whenever you're ready, I'm right here," I told her.

She hesitated a moment, then finally said, "I had my yearly check up a few months ago with my OBGYN. She tested everything from pregnancy to STD's. I'm HIV positive."

I didn't know how to respond, or what to say. Bernice broke down crying by this time. I hugged her neck, and comforted her the way my mother used to do me.

After awhile, when she calmed down I told her that she always would have a friend in me. I let her know that if she ever needed anyone to talk to, I was here.

"Have Lil' Bean been tested? Or did you tell him," I asked?

"Yes, I told him. He's been tested and he's negative. All of my kids are negative too."

"Well who else have you been with?" I asked.

"Mario," she cried.

"You didn't use a condom with him," I asked!

"We started out using condoms, but after it broke once, we just stopped. That's why I pulled the trigger."

I didn't know what to say. My eyes had begun to tear up.

"Bernice, you know to always use a condom."

"I know. I messed up bad. Lil' Bean left me, but he's still my friend. Even though he's negative, he has to return in six months to be tested again. He's a nervous wreck. He moved out, but he still pays all of the bills, and pick the kids up every morning for school. My kids want to know why daddy moved out. Everything is driving me crazy. I don't know what to tell them," she stated.

We talked, and talked, and talked some more. This information made me so aware, and more alert about the choices that I have made in life. It had been awhile since I had my last HIV test done. That was definitely added to my immediate 'To do List'. My new motto would now be, "If you are trying to have unprotected sex with me, then you must already have HIV!" Ladies and gentlemen, please STRAP IT UP!!! For real though, that way you can't go wrong. I always used condoms anyway. With all of my boyfriends in the past, it was never an issue not to use one. I am too young, and too busy living life to let a baby slow me down either. Plus, I'd rather be shot, or stabbed to death before I die of HIV.

Bernice and I finished talking and getting dressed. She knew that she had a friend in me, and that I would always be in her corner no matter what. I told her that even though she was positive, that did not mean that she couldn't live a healthy lifestyle. Hell, look at Magic Johnson. The man looks better and healthier every year. She has children that still need her. I could only imagine how she must have been feeling. It was time to step out and have a drink.

We were finally dressed and ready to walk out of the door. I decided on my new Dolce and Gahanna pants set, silver pumps, and a silver clutch purse. I wore diamond studded hoop earrings, my diamond cut necklace, and matching bracelet to accent the outfit. Bernice was working her outfit too. She wore a green Chanel skirt set, a gold chain belt, and gold pumps, and a large gold and green Chanel bag. We looked and smelled like a million dollars. It was time to turn some heads.

We pulled up in the hottest club in town, Club 2001, and paid twenty dollars to park. The line was wrapped around the building, and there was no way that I was going to stand and wait! We walked over to the V.I.P. line, which was shorter, and paid fifty dollars apiece for entry. The VIP side was much better anyhow because it was less crowded, and more laid back. Plus the baller's always paid VIP.

We were at the bar ordering our first round of drinks when I spotted him. He was standing in the corner, looking down at the lower level of the club. With him was Lil' Mark and a couple of his other homeboys.

"You see you know who over in the corner, right?" Bernice asked.

"I'm not even trying to see him right now."

I could feel them checking us out. The bartender handed us our drinks, and left our tab open. The D.J. played Tupac's, 'Shed so Many Tears,' and the whole club got crunk! By the time they played 'Eightball and M.J.G.'s 'Coming Out Hard,' every nigga in the club was on their feet! We were jamming in our own world.

I don't know why nigga's kept brushing up on my ass every time I danced. They were really getting on my nerves. Can't a Diva look good and dance without being grabbed on??? Nigga's are so bold. What if I walked up to one of them, and just grabbed their dick? At that very moment, someone behind me grabbed a handful of my ass, and put his arms around my waist like he knew me!! Where they do that at? I turned around, ready to swing, and looked up. It was Keston! Now where in the hell did he come from?

"Nigga, keep your hands off of me," I yelled over the

music!

"Whatever. You know this belongs to me," he said while still trying to grab my waist.

"Hold up partner! Didn't she say back the fuck up," Drake yelled stepping in Keston's face.

Before Keston could open his mouth, Drake swung. Drake's whole crew jumped on Keston. I didn't know that Drake had even been looking for this nigga. He'd heard that Keston used to kick my ass. I don't know how he found out because I never told him. They fucked him up, and security carried him out of the door.

"Are you okay Desi?" Drake asked.

"Yeah, thanks," I replied, still trying to get over what just happened.

"You and your girl come over here with us, so I can keep my eye on you guys," he said while grabbing my hand.

"Hold up. We're going to the bathroom first," I replied.

"Alright, I will be right here," Drake said.

I needed to freshen up, and catch my breath. These nigga's are always tripping! Bernice and I walked downstairs to the ladies room. It was super crowded. I still couldn't get over what had just happened!

"That nigga don't play about you," Bernice said.

I was in the mirror checking my make-up, and fixing my hair. Some chick stood beside me and says,

"Don't you have a man, and ain't he locked up? I wish that you would leave me and my man alone."

This was the same bitch that I got into it with at one of Mario's parties awhile ago. This was the same bitch that he came to my job with when he first got out of prison. This broad got nerve! She don't know me like that. It's not my fault that the nigga she wants, wants someone else.

"First of all bitch, if that was your man then he wouldn't be all in my face. Just because your dumb ass let him fuck you when he gets ready, that does not make him your man!" I'm shaking my damn head… "Don't be mad because that nigga loves me," I yelled!

I guess that I struck a nerve or something and this silly broad tried to swing on me. Please tell me where they do that at? I grabbed her fake, Mary J Blige wanna be looking ass by her yellow weave, and banged her face into the mirror, over and over, and over again! Everyone in the bathroom stepped back. I kept banging it until the mirror broke. Then I slung her on the ground and sat on her. I was punching her in the face, and I couldn't stop. All of the frustration that I had built up in me from my mother and everything else just came out. I didn't realize that the girl was bleeding and unconscious.

"Destiny, let's go!" Bernice screamed, trying to pull me up.

At that moment is when I snapped out of it. We left the bathroom just as security was walking in. We went straight out the door, to valet, and got in the truck. It would be a very long time before I went out again.

Drake called me early that next morning asking me what had happened. I told him that his bitch that he's been fucking for awhile, the one that he swore it wasn't nothing, came in my face approaching me about him! I told him exactly what she said and how she had tried me. He told me that he had been kicking it with her since I didn't want to be with him. To me that was some bullshit, because he had been knocking her off for a long time. He told me that she was in the hospital and that they were keeping her overnight for a 23hr observation due to her injuries. The police had come to the hospital to make a report and see if she wanted to press charges. He said that since she didn't know my full name, charges could not be pressed. She was so pissed off at him because he would not tell her my last name. That was a wrap for me and Drake.

Deon would be out in a week. I began starting to accept his collect calls again. I told him everything that had been happening to me. I told him that I had been helping Drake's mother and going over to check on hr. I told him about both of the fights in the club. I told him about everything, except for the one night of passion that Drake and I had. Some things a woman should keep to herself. That was one of them!

I was there at the jail, waiting for my man to come out. He looked sexy as hell even though he had put on a little weight and his skin got a little lighter. My baby was looking good! No wonder that bitch wanted my man.

"Hey baby, I missed you," he said as he walked over to the car.

He hugged and kissed me so long that I had to catch my breath. We left and went straight to the house. Once we were there he took a shower, and changed clothes. The clothes that he had on, he threw them in the garbage, including his shoes. We talked and made love all day. I knew that I had made the right choice.

Over the next couple of days, I had met his entire immediate family, even his kids. Deon had three kids, that all had the same mother. They were raised by his older sister since they were babies. He had two boys and one girl. They were all right behind each other, only a year apart. Dixie was the oldest. I must say that it took a real woman to do what his sister had done. Not only did she do a good job, she did it well. These kids were very respectful. She was ready for a break and I couldn't blame her. She was still young and beautiful, and had no kids of her own. Deon had talked to me about us moving into a larger place and getting the kids. It really didn't seem like such a big deal, it wasn't like I was doing it by myself, their dad was there too. On top of that, I love kids and kids loved me. Almost all of my friends had children too.

I would pick them up and we would hang out. Sometimes we went to the movies, bowling, or out to eat. I enjoyed my weekends with the kids. I had just as much fun as they did! Is that crazy or what? To me it wasn't a problem at all. Less than a month later, Deon, the kids, and I were moving into a three bedroom home. We lived near the Navy base, and we had a huge front and back yard. At the age of nineteen years old, I became an instant live in step mother!

I had quit my job, and still remained in school full time. I obtained the transcripts from the kid's previous schools, and all of their shot records. Within one week all of them were in school. I assigned each of them daily chores. Beds had to be made before they went to school in the mornings, and homework was to be do as soon as they got out of school. There was no going outside to play afterschool if your chores were not done. I cooked, cleaned, and washed clothes for the entire household. I attended PTA meetings and was present at all school activities. My schedule was set. I was home as soon as class was done because I had too much shit to do. On the weekends Deon and I would do things together, but we mostly did things as a family, all five of us. All of my friends thought that I had bumped my head. They thought I was crazy, or that he had voodoo on me or something. They could not believe that I, having no kids of my own, would even consider taking care of three kids that wasn't mine! I was in love and actually enjoying my family life. I loved his kids just as much as I loved him; we all lived great together and ate well too. We had everything that we needed.

Almost one year had passed since I heard from Drake. He called my cell phone one day to let me know that his mom had passed. I could hear the pain in his voice. Tears had begun to form in my eyes. It hurt me to hear him in so much pain. He sounded so sad over the phone. He let me know that he felt like that I should know. The funeral was to be held next week.

"Would it be okay if I come?" I asked him.

"Come on now Destiny, what kind of question is that?"

"I don't know. I didn't know if you hated me, or was still mad at me," I slowly replied.

"I could never hate you, how could you think something like that? Destiny I will always love you no matter what. Plus, you know that my mom would want you to be there."

"I am so sorry about your mother," I sadly replied.

"Thanks. You know that she loved you right? I don't know how I'm going to make it without her. I just gotta get away. I'm not sure where I'm going, but I got to leave here," he said.

I could tell that he was hurting bad. I would keep him in my prayers; I fully understood his pain.

CHAPTER 20

Deon was going out of town more frequently. The more he went, the more I worried. I worried about him being pulled over, and I also worried about the haters and the snitches. In Pensacola, they were giving life sentences just for conspiracy. Lacy was a living testimony to that. You did not have to get caught with shit. All it took was for a lame ass, snitch ass hater to get on the witness stand and point you out. That shit was crazy to me! The state were giving females, who didn't do shit but spend the money, just as much time! My biggest concern for him was the highway, and a possible trafficking charge. His chances were increased especially since he was a black man, and riding by himself, come on now, everybody knows about the RWB, riding while black charge.

One day I asked Deon if he thought that it looked better if a male and female was in the car together.

"Yeah, maybe so, but I can't let you take that risk with me," he replied.

"Baby, if it helps you, then it helps us. Next time you take that trip, I am going too. I can also help you drive," I replied!

After I snapped on him several times, he finally gave in.

From that moment on, we would drive to the bottom together. We would shop, eat, and kick it while we were there. I never knew the extent of how much weight that he actually had up until this point. I knew now. We were like Bonnie and Clyde all the way.

We were in love with each other, and life was good! We had each other's back no matter what. I was his hood and college girl chick. He was my best friend and my nigga. There was no room for the gold digging ass broads, and no one could tell me about my man. Trust me when I tell you, those broads were all on his dick. You know that your girl was not having it though!

Star and I did not talk that much lately. She was still with my brother-n-law, and she was catching hell. My sister was pregnant with her first child. This was the first child for both of them period. I didn't understand why this nigga was even cheating on her in the first place. It was crazy! The chick that he was cheating on her was like five, No, make that ten notches below her. Star was his ride or die chick. When I say that, I mean, Ms. Lady loved him unconditionally! She was smart, responsible, and loyal. She was not a gold digger, because she got her own. Her intelligence meant that there has to be a 5yr, nope a 10yr plan. Why are men so stupid? No, let me take that back. All men are not stupid, because everybody does not have those same issues. The bitch that he was cheating with was like five notches below Star though! Why do nigga's do that? Shamar and Deon were opposites. They were totally opposites, like day and night. Star is my sister, and that is my baby girl. She is very sociable, and gets along with everyone in the family. She didn't deserve to be treated like that.

There was only a select few in the family that I actually dealt with, period. The ones that I didn't deal with, I did not fuck with them at all. The ones that I did not deal with would say that I was stuck up, or had an attitude. I call them fans. They would ask me stupid questions like, "Where Did I get my outfit from? Or, who did my hair? No this is the killer, "Didn't you just get your hair done?"

Why in the hell were they all in my business? They would say that Deon should have been with Star, and that I should have been with Shamar. My personality could have never dealt with the shit that Shamar was dishing out. No, not never! My man loved me, and he was at home every night. We had a great relationship!

Now don't get me wrong, there were times where we did argue. It was mostly over stupid things, like leaving his things lying around, or what we were going to eat for dinner. We did get into a couple of big arguments though. I would put him out until I had a chance to calm down. Either way, my kids had to stay! I took my kids everywhere with me. Hell, I enjoyed their company. I was crazy about them in a major way. I knew that they all loved me too, but there would be times when I would get into it with my step-daughter.

My step-sons' were like "Yes Ma'am, and no Ma'am". No not Shia! She was more like, 'What', or 'My daddy said this'… As the only little girl, she had her daddy wrapped around her little finger, and she knew it. She would start arguments between us for her own reasons! Everyone saw it but him. I would get so mad at him for being so blind! I could not understand why, if I saw it then why couldn't he see it too? The boys would get chastised for something that they did, but when it came to her, she would only get a slap on the wrist. She knew how to play her daddy and she did it well.

When things got too out of hand, I would call her Aunt who raised them. Trust me when I tell you, they did not want her to get all up in that ass! They feared and respected her. They also loved their mother to death, even though she did not raise them. Once the kids hung up the phone with either one of them, their attitudes were totally different. Eventually my stepdaughter grew on me, and I on her. I guess she saw that I wasn't going anywhere and I loved them just as much as I loved their dad. You know that kids are able to sense when they are sincerely loved. Once she finally opened up to me, she told me everything. I love all of my babies, and it made me feel good to receive the same love in return.

Two years had passed since we first got the kids. I had taken a break from school and had only two semesters to complete in order to obtain my Associates in Science degree. Everything was still going well, but at some point, I was starting to feel closed in. I missed hanging with my girls, I missed doing my own thing, and most of all, I missed my freedom. Not freedom to be, or hang around other men. I just missed the freedom to do whatever it was that I wanted to do.

The more time we spent together, the more Deon had started pressuring me to get married. I wasn't ready to get married just yet, hell, I was only twenty-one years old! I knew that I had been through a lot, but in my mind there was a whole world out there that I had not seen yet. Then, on the other hand, maybe that is what I needed… I don't know… I mean, Deon is a good man, a good friend, a good father, and a great provider. What else could a girl ask for? But in my heart I knew that there was something that I was missing. I haven't figured it out yet, maybe you can tell me... I was tired of sitting in the house, I was tired of being a mom, and I was getting tired of being a house wife. There was a huge, big and exciting world out there with plenty of places to travel to, and exciting people to meet, right? The left side of my brain was screaming "Hell No!" At the end of the day, reality set in, and the reality was that I loved my man and I wasn't about to let him go. He told me that if we didn't get married, that we needed to go our own separate ways. Oh hell to the No! There were too many bitches that would love to have my man, and there was no way that I was going to hand him to them on a silver platter. These females were at him all the time, but I took pride in the fact that he only had eyes for me, Destiny. Even though I wasn't ready to get married, I wasn't read to let him go.

CHAPTER 21

We had a nice church wedding in downtown Orlando. The morning of the wedding, everyone was at the church. All of his family members flew down, and everyone that lived here attended. Some of my family and friends came down as well. The closer that it got to the last moment of officially being settled down and a wife, I think that I started getting what they call "Cold Feet." Everything had already been planned, set up, and paid for. My step-daughter helped me pick out a beautiful wedding dress, we bought her the most adorable brides' maid dress, and my step sons looked really good in their suits. La'Mica was my best friend and maid of honor. Everything seemed picture perfect. Deon's best friend's wife, Linda, had set up the entire event. She even went all out on the reception too. Why was I even tripping? I was so nervous, that I didn't know how to respond or act.

While everyone was at the church waiting on me, I was at home, sitting at the computer playing solitaire. All the while, my phone is blowing up! Should I, or shouldn't I? That is the question…. Okay, if I win this last hand of solitaire, then I would go. If I lost then it wasn't meant to be… Damn, I won. The limo driver was still waiting outside.

Linda had done an excellent job planning this

wedding. I was in awe! Everything was perfect, all the way down to the smallest detail. She hired a professional photographer, assisted with the decorations, and the food was off the chain! I must say that the photographer did his thing. Our pictures came out beautifully. Deon and I exchanged vows and said, "I do." I was officially a married woman.

Everything had changed in our house after that. It was the same but different. It's hard to explain. Our relationship deteriorated after we got married. We started arguing more. Everything was an argument. We had only been married for three months. I was about to go crazy. I wanted to get away. La'Mica and I started going out a lot. Deon would be pissed off when I came home at three and four o'clock in the morning. I was a grown woman and he was not my daddy. This was an every weekend thing. We hit every party in Orlando. I had got a job at Sprint PCS working in the activation department. I worked Monday through Friday from 9 am – 6 pm. Some weekends I would have my bag packed on Friday morning and leave work and go straight to La'Mica's house to get ready for our weekend partying. We had started partying in Miami every weekend. We would go to shop and have a good time. We would stay on the beach and just ball out of control. This was the life that I wanted to live "The Single Life".

Deon had started following me during the week. He thought I had another man. I truly didn't. I would just socialize and converse with men, but I didn't sleep with anyone. My goodies were precious and you had to earn the right just to peek at it. I wasn't cheating but I didn't want to be married anymore. If I wanted to creep I couldn't. Deon knew every real nigga on every block. I had to get away. I knew that I couldn't leave him and live in the same city. Something had to give.

We had been married six months now and each and every day was worse than the day before. We constantly argued and there was no trust in this marriage. This was not healthy for me, Deon or the kids. I was on my way home from work one day and passed by the local military recruiting stations. I immediately made a sharp u-turn at the next intersection. As I pulled into the parking lot I read the sign on the building, "Navy, Air force & Army." I walked in the Air Force first. I had heard they were the best choice out of all the branches of services to go into. The recruiter inside that office was acting funny and looking down at me. He told me that they couldn't accept me into the Air Force with all the gold fronts in my mouth. Fuck ya'll! I yelled. I went into the next office. They were friendly. I took the pre-ASVAB right there and I aced it with flying colors. The officer's asked if I could return the next day so that I could take the qualifying exam and physical evaluation. I told the officer that I had been smoking and I knew that I would test positive for marijuana. He asked me if I minded riding to the store with him so that we could fix the issue of me possibly testing positive. I was like, "sure no problem." We went to an herbal store about 10 minutes away from the recruiter's station. He purchased a juice that cost $60 and gave me the instructions on how to use it. The next day after my work shift I notified my supervisor of my plans to join the military and she gave me the next three days off. The recruiter drove me to Jacksonville, Florida which is where the nearest Military Entrance Processing Station (MEPS). The first day I took the physical examination. This consisted of a pap smear, blood work, A.I.D.S testing, body measurements and simple movement exercises. I was good in all areas. We were taken back to a nearby hotel to stay the night. The following morning a shuttle bus was there to pick us up to take us back to the MEPS receiving location. Now it was time for the written testing the ASVAB. The ASVAB is a multiple-aptitude battery that measures developed abilities and helps predict future academic and occupational success in the military. It has been at least a year since I had been in school, but I was sure that I could handle it. It was a multiple choice testing process. How hard can it be? The requirements were to score at least a 33 and I scored a 56. My highest scoring area was in numbers. During the job selection processing I selected a job as a dispersing clerk (DK). In the civilian world that's equivalent to a payroll, human resources and accounting clerk. I had sworn in and was to leave in three days to go to basic training.

The next day reality had kicked in. "Destiny, what the fuck did you just do!" I asked myself. I had never thought about going into the service before. Of all the people I know this was not expected. I loved getting my hair and nails done and dressing up to much. I loved coming and going as I pleased and being my own boss. Now I was going to be taking orders from people I didn't know. "Hold on!" I thought let me call this recruiter back and let him know I was just playing. When the recruiter heard me out he let me know that if I didn't show up that they would come looking for me and it wouldn't be a civilized situation. I had to break the news to Deon. When I told my husband that I would be leaving in two days he was devastated. "How are you going to join the service and we just got married six months ago?" he asked. He was right and I didn't want to go. I told him I was sorry and it was too late. I stayed at home the next two days. I called my job back and told them that I wouldn't be returning.

Boot camp was hell, but "Me" Destiny, I'm a survivor. I take it how it comes. It was kind of fucked up that my recruiter didn't tell me anything on what to expect. I went in blind as a bat. I had packed up a roll-on luggage bag that had to be sent back. I was physically out of shape, my chest full of blunts and cigarettes. The very first week was hectic. We were issued uniforms and our hair had to be cut to one inch above our collar. Everyone had to go to the dentist and all wisdom teeth were pulled immediately. We all had to learn how to march together as a unit. Breakfast was served at four thirty every morning and all beds had to be perfectly made. Uniforms had to be worn in accordance to military guidelines. If one person broke a rule or fell below standards, we were all held accountable for our fellow shipmate

After being there for one week they threw everyone on the track. We had to run one and a half miles within thirteen minutes. This was a huge problem for me. The only place I ran is from the house to my car. Period. I tried, I tried and I tried some more. We were told that if we stopped we would be considered disqualified. My shipmates were trying to push me by cheering me on saying, "Come on Moore, you can do it!" These were the people that I got off the same bus with from the airport and arrived to the base with from day one. We were all afraid of the unknown. We all made a connection and a small bond began to form within the group. No one wanted anyone to fail. My chest burned badly. I couldn't do it anymore, so I stopped. I was set back one week until I met the requirement of completing my run in thirteen minutes. Boot camp was nine weeks for me instead of the standard 8 weeks. I passed each and every obstacle after that because I was determined to not be set back again. Boot camp was finally over and my military graduation ceremony was in three days.

Deon had flown in to Great Lakes, Illinois for my graduation. I was so proud of myself. I had made it! I was especially proud when I looked up and saw Deon as I walked across the stage. I just keep surprising myself. I had never expected to be in or join any branch of the Armed Forces. After the ceremony, Deon and I talked about where I would be stationed for duty. It was very apparent how much he and the kids missed me. Deon has always been a family man so it came to no surprise when he expressed his love for me. No man had ever loved me the way that Deon did. Boot camp turned out to be a very positive experience for me. It gave me a totally different outlook on life. It taught me to appreciate the simple things like waking up in the morning, the quality of time verses the quantity of time, and valuing my freedom. I was looking at life with a whole knew set of eyes and it felt good. Within two days I had to fly to Meridian, Mississippi to report for duty at the school of aviation and training for eight weeks. I hated this place. I hated everything about it. It was a redneck, hick ass, country ass town and the base was miles away from any of the main stores and malls. The people in the town seemed very behind on current times. Thank God, I only had to be there for eight weeks. It was somewhat the same routine as Boot camp, but way more laid back. Breakfast was still at four thirty in the morning and physical training, P.T., was a requirement right after breakfast.

Following P.T. were classes and after classes we would head back to the barracks to study. Sometimes I called home or sometimes I would stand outside and have a smoke in the smoking area. I got along well with all the fellas in a big sister kind of way. To me the base was like a big college campus. Everybody was sleeping with everybody and I was not with that. Most of these young people had never been away from home or were straight out of high school and didn't know how to act. I always tried to teach them a little something and tell them something good so they called me "Momma Moore" because they said I had an old soul. The females on the other hand couldn't stand me. They hated the fact that I got along so well with the dudes they were sleeping with. If they would have stepped back a second and listened to me, I would have told them that they didn't have to sleep with these guys to get them to like them. The first half of the game is the physical attraction and obviously that part is already there. The second half of the game is your mental attraction, or how you carry yourself. These females were young and dumb. They had to learn on their own.

The eight weeks seemed to drag by, but I finally completed my training. I was now awaiting my duty orders to find out my next location. When the announcement came through of where I was to be stationed, I could have fell to the floor and cried. When I tell you that I could have hit the floor, I could have hit the floor! I was being stationed for the next four years, right there in Meridian, Mississippi. I did not join the fucking Navy to stay in any part of Mississippi. I could have stayed in Orlando for this. OH, HELL NO! I found out quick that there was absolutely nothing I could do about it. I belonged to Uncle Sam now. Since I had to be there, I decided to make the best out of it. I mean what other choice did I have? I had my husband bring me my car. He had put rims on it since I'd been gone and it made my car look totally different to me. The military police, M.P.'s, would pull me over all the time, asking how could I afford a car like this and I was only an E-2. I guess they saw the gold in my mouth and they type of car that I drove and automatically assumed drugs. On the weekends, I would fly home and visit my husband. It never failed every time I returned to the base they would drug test me. I think that I was the only on the base that got tested every week. The standard was once a month. I was so sick of this stereotyping shit. I wasn't even smoking at all. I got just as much hate from the broads on the base too. These dumb hoes couldn't stand me. They would say that I thought that I was all this and all that. Hell, whatever I did they should be doing too? Why shouldn't they think that they were all that. If they didn't feel that way about themselves, then who in the hell would? It's not my fault that they have self-esteem issues. This materialistic shit didn't mean anything to me. I did not join the service for the money, or to get nice things. I already had that, plus a husband who loved me. What makes you feel good about yourself and what makes you feel complete has to come from within and that's what I was searching for.

I had been there in Meridian for two years now and was used to the routine. I knew what to do and how to get around some of the rules. I had started to hang out at a local sports bar regularly. One week night after hanging out at the sports bar watching a fight I tried to tip toe back into my barracks room undetected. The Military

Police were doing their rounds and spotted me trying to sneak in. They took me to the Officer on Deck to report in, which was the way that I was suppose to report. It's their duty to log all activities that take place on the grounds while on duty. I was ordered to take a breathalyzer and sent to my room. I was sent to the Captain's Mass, which is the military court system the following week. I was put on restriction for 60 days without pay. I was embarrassed by the fact that they placed me on restriction like a child.

Two weeks later, another chick gets into trouble for the same reason and was found guilty of the same charges as I was, but her sentence was a lot harsher. It was ruled that she would be busted down in rank and sentence to the fleet undesignated which was less money & no job title. She knew of my outcome and started to complain. She argued that it wasn't fair that I was given a lighter sentence for the same exact charges and that she would argue her claim all the way up the chain of command. After her threats of challenging the sentencing my charges were increased to match the charges given to her and I was scheduled to be sent to a ship, without a specific job title. OH, HELL NO!!! Where they do that at? I didn't do hard labor work before I came into the Navy and I sure as hell wasn't about to start. I felt like they were putting me through double jeopardy, and that they shouldn't be able to change my sentence after I had already been sentenced. Since the Navy wanted to play dirty I wasn't going to stick around to waddle in the mud. I went A.W.O.L better known as absent with out leave. I got in my car and drove right off the base.

As I made my great escape I went from city to city all down the Gulf Coast to Central Florida, clubbing. I picked up my Aunt Donna from Biloxi, Mississippi and we balled out of control. We stayed a couple of nights at a casino hotel in Biloxi, we partied in Pascagoula and then stayed a few nights in Mobile just partying. We left there and kicked it in Pensacola a few nights and then we headed over into Jacksonville where the party really went down. We stayed a week in Jacksonville then made our way down to Orlando. When I arrived home I told Deon what had happened. He told me that I had to go back. I knew that, but I was going to have some fun first. I told him that I was leaving the next day to go back to face my fate. After spending time with my family I got up the next morning to head back to Meridian, MS. Well, that's what I told Deon. I didn't go anywhere. I went and got a hotel on International Drive and balled out of control. I had been in Orlando almost a week before Aunt Donna and I decided to leave. We made the same detours on our way back, stopping in each town again. I had been missing for the base for 29 days. One more day and I would have been sent to the brig, military jail for my excursion across state lines. I was given the option to accept my charges that were presented before I left or to get out on an administrative discharge with eligibility for re-enlistment. I chose the administrative discharge. I remained in Meridian for six more months then they released me to go back to Orlando. I wasn't home for a full week before I got a job at the local hospital in the admitting department making more money than when I was enlisted in the Navy. Now ain't that some shit? Isn't it crazy how life works, I thought to myself. My husband was happy to have me home. We were going to try to make our marriage work.

My home girl La'Mica was having issues with her

man. They shared an apartment and worked at the same place. La'Mica was secretive about her relationships and always had been. You never knew what was going on with her until the shit hit the fan. That's my sister and I love her to death. If she needed me for anything I would be there. That's why when she called and said she needed to get away, my door was wide open. She had temporarily moved in with me, Deon and the kids.

This was all a bad idea for Deon though. La'Mica and I partied every weekend and Deon hated it. We would leave on Friday after work and would be gone until Sunday evening. One particular weekend that we went to Miami, we stayed three days instead of two. We left on Thursday afternoon and got a room on the beach. It was Memorial Day weekend. Every year this weekend was off the chain. Nigga's came from everywhere! The malls and highways were packed. People were in town from everywhere and anywhere. Every time we came to Miami we had a ball. We went to the festival during the day and the clubs at night. We went to every mall in the city and we left that Sunday afternoon trying to beat the traffic. It actually wasn't that bad. We made it back home in good timing. We got back to the hotel, showered and changed our clothes before we checked out. I had an idea "Let's go to the Palladium, since it's kind of early," I said to La'Mica. It was only 10 o'clock and I really wasn't ready to go home. "I don't know Destiny, I'm kind of tired," She replied. I was able to persuade her though before we passed the exit to get there.

We were only in the club for about an hour before La'Mica was ready to go. "Come on La'Mica! The club is just starting to get crunk," I pouted. She wasn't having it. She was ready to go. "You can go ahead, I will find a ride home," I told her. I knew too many people and this was my spot, I knew I could find a ride home. I was looking good and turning heads all night. I had a new outfit and shoes on that I had just gotten from the Bermuda Mall. You couldn't tell me shit! I met a baller named Tony. We conversed all night and he didn't let me out of his sight. The waitress kept coming with rounds of Patron. He said that he wanted to get to know me and would take me home. Tony and I were vibing with each other the entire ride to my house. I had him park three houses down in an empty driveway. We were chilling in the car smoking a blunt just listening to *Granddaddy Souf's* new c.d.; it was off the chain! Tony asked me if I had a man. I told him that I was in a situation and things weren't going right. All of a sudden we hear a loud BANG! Then glass shattered everywhere. His car was surrounded by thugs. He drove a completely refurbished Chevy Caprice Classic sitting on 20 inch rims, leather seats, and candy paint with suicide doors. Tony was forced out of his car at gun point and pushed on the ground. My window was all the way down, so the thugs on my side are trying to grab my purse. These nigga's got me fucked up! I refused to be violated in my own neighborhood where I pay rent. I went the fuck off. I was yelling and screaming while playing tug-of-war with my purse while all of this is going on, Tony is laid out on the ground stripped of his jewelry, money and shoes. Everything was happening so fast. One of the hoodlums jumps in the car with me and backs out of the driveway. I am driven from my neighborhood and kidnapped while Tony was left on the ground. I am still going off as the driver is going 100 miles per hour on the highway. I take off my high heel shoe and start beating him in the face with it. He grabs my shoe and throws it out the window. I pull off my other shoe and go after him again. "Get out the car, you stupid bitch," he yells. How the fuck did he expected me to get the fuck out? I was in a rage as I started kicking him across the seat with my feet. I yelled, "YOU GET THE FUCK OUT THE CAR!" He started slamming on the brakes to throw me off the seat. I had no idea where we were headed. He finally pulls up in front of a church in what seemed to be a quiet neighborhood. As soon as the car stops I jumped out and started running. I see headlights up the road in front of me. I ran towards the head lights. "Someone help! Please," I yelled. The car pulled up to me and I ran to the driver's side. My heart dropped to the ground. It was the rest of the crew from the house. It had to be at least seven or eight of them. They surrounded me and began to beat me. I stood up and fought until I couldn't fight anymore. I was balled up on the ground when a gun is stuck in my mouth. "Shoot that bitch, shoot that bitch," one of them yelled. I thought I was dead already. Then one of them said, "Naw, leave her alone." Just like that they all walked away and got into their car including Tony's car. My guardian angel had saved me again. Thank you Lord!

It was four o'clock in the morning and I am walking from door to door. With no avail I still had my purse. I was afraid they were gonna change their minds and come back to finish me off. My face is bloody; both my eyes are swollen and black. Every inch of my body ached in pain. I wasn't going to make it far walking. I prayed that someone, anyone would open the door to help me. Every door that I knocked on the people would yell and tell me to get away from the door. Why were they doing this to me? The forth door I found sympathy. She didn't open the door, but she dialed 9-1-1. She told me to stay right there and she would get the police. It took them 20 minutes to respond. That was the longest twenty minutes of my life. They finally arrived and I made a report. I was taken back to my house where the police were already there investigating the crime scene. Tony had caught the city bus to the local police precinct. The ambulance was called and I refused medical treatment. The hospital they were assigned to was the local hospital where I worked in the emergency room. I didn't want the people that I saw everyday to see me like this. I signed a release form and vowed to see my private physician in the morning. I checked in with my doctor and he sent me to have x-rays and blood work done. He fussed at me for not going to the emergency room for treatment earlier that morning. I received a prescription for the pain and an excuse from work for two weeks. The event played over and over in my head. I wanted to talk to Tony to see how he was feeling, but I didn't have his number. It was in my cell phone which had fallen out of my purse in the car during the struggle. The investigating officer contacted me almost everyday in regards to any details about the case. I had called my cell phone provider to find out all the numbers that were dialed since that night. There were lots of calls made. I had begun calling some of the numbers back to try and get any information from the people that they had called. No one talked. I called the officer and told him that I had a list of numbers that maybe could find a lead from there. At that point we had no motive and no suspects. I also asked if he had any contact information for Tony. He said yes. He gave me Tony's home telephone number. "I'll follow up on this list of numbers and get back to you as soon as possible," he said before hanging up the phone.

The following morning I called Tony. I was about to hang up then he answered on the forth ring. "Is this Tony?" I asked.

"Yeah, who is this?" he asked.

"Destiny." There was a silence. "Hello," I asked. I wasn't sure if the phone had disconnected or he was just holding the phone.

"Yeah, what up?" he asked.

"I just wanted to talk to you and see if you were okay."

"Look here Lil Momma, I don't know what kind of games you playing, but I ain't that nigga to be fucking with," he said.

"Hold the fuck up, I don't know what you are talking about but those nigga's stuck a gun in my mouth, those nigga's almost killed me," I yelled back

"What?"

"Hell yeah! All those nigga's jumped me and stomped me and then left me for dead. My face is fucked up and I can't go to work for at least two weeks," I told him. He couldn't believe it. None of those things had happen to him. I guess I pissed them off with my big mouth. I guess it wasn't supposed to go like that, if I had cooperated like he did. Tony had given me the directions to his house, which was on the outskirts of Orlando. It took me about 30 minutes to get there. He walked out the house to meet me as soon as I pulled in the driveway. He thought that I had set him up. He said all of his friends called him a fool. It did appear that way though. We were parked in front of an empty house and I leave with the nigga's. I don't think that he really trusted me to come to his house. I didn't know what kind of trap he had waiting for me when I got there. Maybe he was going to kill me or kick my ass. I didn't know. All I know is that I wanted him to see my face so he could see for himself that I suffered more than he did. Yeah, he lost his car and they took his money, but I almost lost my life. I took my Dolce and Gabbana shades off as I walked towards him. He stood there frozen. I was fucked up! I looked like a victim of a hate crime.

"Man no! Man no!" is all that he kept saying.

We were still cool after that, but that's it. We talked on the phone some, but it was mostly related to the case. His cell phone had been taken that night too and calls had been made from his number. I had him call his cell phone provider and have them fax a list of the number's that were dialed since that night. I gave him the detective's fax number to send the information directly over to his desk. I thought to myself, "Why didn't the detective make this the first thing he did in the case," especially since we didn't have anything else to go on. Oh well, I thought to myself, whatever it's going to take to catch the bastards. They were going to pay for what they did to me. Two weeks later, after returning to work I received a phone call from the detective wanting to meet with me after work. We met at a restaurant close to my job, Bahama Breeze. I ordered an appetizer and sweet tea. He then informed me on the progress of the case. Apparently, the perpetrators went to a young lady's house after the incident. She placed a phone call from one of the cell phones to Atlanta, GA. The detective was able to do a call back to the number and an unidentified male answered the phone. The guy was then questioned whether or not he knew anybody in Orlando. He informed the detective that he was in the area a year before for a church convention and only knew one person personally in the city. Her name was Sonya, and she was only seventeen years old. The detective contacted Sonya and paid her a visit. Come to find out, both her parents were pastors and had no idea that she had boys in their home that night. Sonya started singing like a bird. She knew all four of the nigga's that attacked me. The detective pulled out ten photographs for me to identify my attackers. Within the next three months, all four were arrested at different times and different places. Dummies! They were caught all because of a cell phone. There charges ranged from armed robbery; kidnapping; aggravated assault; carjacking; arson because the car had been found stripped down, burnt up and sitting on bricks; and attempted murder. They each got twenty years without parole.

CHAPTER 22

It started to become more and more evident that my marriage was not going to work. My step-children were suffering from the affects of our relationship. Deon and I constantly argued. I was too busy running the streets and he was busy following behind me. They were not getting the attention that they needed and deserved. My fifteen year old step-daughter had gotten pregnant and we didn't even know that she was having sex. She hid her pregnancy from us for four months with no prenatal care. She went to visit her mom one weekend and her mom noticed her stomach. She was changing clothes when her mom walked into the room. Her mom couldn't believe it. They sat down and had a mother/daughter talk. She remained with her mom for the next few months. I was dealing with too much stress. I need a break! I was only 23 years old and I too young for this shit. La'Mica and I had moved into a two bedroom apartment as roommates. It was so quiet and peaceful. We both worked different shifts and different days. It was very seldom that we were at home at the same time. It was a real nice apartment in a good location. It was near the mall and lots of shopping plazas. It also wasn't to far from our jobs. We got along great and life was much more simple. Just when I thought things couldn't get any better, Deon started stalking and

harassing me. He would sit and park his car outside in the
parking lot just waiting to see if anyone was coming to
my house. He would stay at the door for hours knocking.
If he saw my car outside he would come to my bedroom
window saying he wanted his wife back. He would check
my voicemail on my cell phone. Hell! I didn't even know
he knew the pass code to my phone. He was starting to
show up at places that I would be. I would be
embarrassed by him and talk to him like shit. I treated
him very badly. Eventually he finally stopped stalking
my house. The next few months I worked my ass off,
taking all the overtime that I could. There were some pay
periods that I worked over 100 hours. I was trying to
stack all the paper that I could. I no longer had Deon to
depend on. I was all on my own this time. I was still
straight though. Even though I was always clubbing and
going out of town when we were together I always made
it a point to save money. Deon and I had separate
accounts and I didn't have to pay any bills in the house
except my cell phone bill. When I would try to help on
the bills he would tell me to put it in the bank. Now that I
had to pay my own bills I wanted to make sure that I was
able to save money and spend the way I was accustom to
doing in the past. I was wise though. If my checking
account would fall low I would stop spending and stack
paper.

I decided to hang out with one of my home girls one
weekend. It had been awhile since I had been anywhere.
Now this bitch knew everybody. She was the queen of all
types of hustles. She boosted, ran check scams, did taxes
and credit card schemes. The bitch was good at what she
did! She wanted to stop in Richmond Heights to holla at
one of her homeboys. We got out the car and stood

outside just kicking it with the fellas. Nigga's were rolling blunts, and there was a huge bottle of Remy Martin V.S.O.P. Now that's what I'm talking about. We were smoking good and drinking good too. "Do you see Stevie checking you out?" asked Mimi. I looked over at a tall, sexy ass, bald headed, nice looking chocolate brother. He didn't have to try hard because his confidence showed just by the way he carried himself. He didn't have a gold grill or anything. Hell, he didn't need anything extra. I couldn't take my eyes off of him. This brother was smooth as hell. Nigga's was jumping when he said something. You could tell who was calling the shots over in his click. Damn, I wanted that man! His demeanor was calm, cool, and collected; however you could tell that he could be ruthless at the same damn time. This man did not play games. He was well known and respected in the area. The rumor was that he had plenty of women and was straight up about it. I walked over to where he was standing and started hollering at him. Right from the jump we were cool. We exchanged numbers and our connection grew from there. Stevie and I had lots of fun together, I mean lots of fun! We would go to the theme parks and we stayed going out to eat and catching the latest movie at the theater. I stopped working so much overtime just so that I could kick it with him. I really liked this guy. I had one big problem with him though, he was married.

I was still in my early twenties and Stevie was a grown man in his early thirties with responsibilities other than himself. Stevie and his wife were high school sweethearts. I think that they were still together out of convenience, or maybe they were just content with one another's ways. He never discussed his life at home with his wife and I didn't question them either. I did wonder though, how could a woman let a brother like Stevie stay out all night. Word on the street was that they had a crazy past and their relationship was basically over. Whatever it was, I didn't feel bad because he was doing all of the creeping before I came into the picture. We did everything together. There was nothing that I couldn't talk to him about or do in front of him. I was in love again. To me Stevie was my soul mate. In the bedroom he was no chump either. Oh, My! We were both some freaks in the sheets. He brought all the freakiness out of me. I didn't know that I could be so freaky. We were more than just "lovers and friends" that would have been an understatement. After a year long courtship the lease on my apartment was over with. La'Mica was pregnant and moving back in with her boyfriend. I had moved in the same apartment complex into a one bedroom apartment. Stevie was over there all the time. I think that was his home away from home. If I wasn't hanging out with my home girls, I was waiting on Stevie. I saw him almost every day, but there were times when I didn't see him for a couple of days. This was starting to bother me. I began to get tired of being number two. I wanted someone that was all mine. Stevie was good to me but I wanted more. Deon had spoiled me financially and emotionally. It was always all about me.

On the days that I didn't see Stevie my girl Mimi would come and keep me company. She kept me updated on everything that went on around town. She told me that Deon had a new woman, and that they were living together. She had three kids and Deon was taking care of her and her children. Please tell me why did I instantly get jealous? I wanted to know who, what, when, and where. Of course Mimi knew all of that. It wouldn't be long before I knew too, especially fucking with Mimi's crazy ass. I found out that the girl name was Fiona and she was two years younger than me. She already had three kids and was straight from the projects. She didn't own a high school diploma or even hold down a fulltime job. She grew up in the projects and had a project mentality. She was known for writing bad checks and using fake names. This was a real loser type of broad, known in the hood as a "Dirty Foot". Her appearance was even worse. She was tall. I mean this check stood three times taller than Deon's short ass. Fiona was dark skinned, heavy set and sloppy looking. I had to confront Deon on this chick. After work tomorrow I was going by the projects. Mimi and I headed over to the projects and rode around in a circle before we finally parked in the driveway. I knew he was in there because I saw his truck and car parked outside. Mimi urged me to cut the car off because she was about to go and knock on the door. I wasn't about to let her confront them alone so I said, "No, you stay right here, I got this. Just watch my back," I replied. I knocked three times before she answered the door. "Is my husband here?" I asked. She looked me up and down. Yeah I'm that bitch, I thought to myself. Man, this chick was ugly as hell. I later found out that it wasn't her outside that he liked her for, but what was on the inside. I guess beauty is only skin deep. After staring me up and down, she told me to hold on, and went into the house.

Ten minutes later, he came to the door. He was shocked as hell. "What you are doing here? he asked. "Deon, we need to talk," I said

"Talk about what Destiny, it's been over a year, what

do we have to talk about? I used to pray to God to send my wife back, but you never came. I've moved on now. I still love you, but I won't be hurt by you again," he said. "Deon, we are still married. Do you wanna throw everything away? I/m sorry, I made a mistake, I still love you too, I told him. He gave me his number, and I put it in my cell phone. He told me to call him tomorrow afternoon on my lunch break, so we could talk.

I gave him a call the next day and we hooked up after work. We met at the Orlando Ale Steak House. We talked about our feelings towards one another and the mistakes that we both had made. I knew that my husband still loved me, I saw it all in his eyes. After dinner and a couple of drinks we followed each other to the Marriott Hotel on International Drive. We made sweet and passionate love all night long. He told me that he was coming home to his wife.

The following morning we went our separate ways. I had to go home and change before work. I called Deon all day from work with no answer in return. His cell kept going straight to voicemail. What the hell was going on? Two days passed and still no word from Deon. Okay, I got something for his ass. I called Kane, the pastor that married us. Kane and Deon had known each other for years. Their families grew up together and Deon had a great deal of respect for Kane. We were members of his church when we attended church together as a family. If Deon would listen to anyone it would be him. I told Kane everything. I also told him that I wanted things to get on the right track in my marriage. Kane did not approve of him shacking up with another woman. Kane told me that we would go over next week, because he had to go out of town tomorrow. "That's cool, just call me as soon as you get back," I told him before hanging up. I was still upset and hurt that Deon had lied to me. Hell no, I wasn't waiting until next week me and Mimi was going over there tomorrow.

It was Saturday morning at ten o'clock when I pulled up in front of Mimi's house. I wanted to go early before they left for the day. Thank you God, both cars were in the drive-way. He was going to tell me what's up. I knocked on the door again. They must have seen me pull up, because both of them stepped outside.

"What do you want Destiny?" he asked.

"What the hell do you mean, what I want? You didn't ask me that while we were having sex," I said. "Did you tell your girl-friend that you were coming home," I asked. "What?" Fiona asked.

"Fiona, I don't know what she's talking about, she is lying," he pleaded.

I think it was an instant reflex because before I knew it, I had swung and hit him dead in the face. He tried to run in the house, but I was right behind him and Fiona was behind me. We fought like cats and dogs in that house. Shit was falling and breaking everywhere. He wouldn't hit me back; he just tried to hold me down so that I would calm down and stop swinging. I was like a mad woman, he couldn't hold me. I looked over at one of Fiona's children screaming in the background and that made me take a chill pill. I realized I was acting a fool at the expense of innocent children. I regained my composure and walked out of the door. As I was leaving, she yelled "Don't come back to my damn house anymore!" Mimi was standing right there at the front door watching everything. "Whatever Hoe", Mimi yelled back at Fiona, as we got into the car to leave. We drove to the near by corner store to talk about what just happen.

"Are you okay girl?" asked Mimi

"Yeah, I just can't believe that he did it like that," I said. I picked up the pone and dialed Kane's number. I broke down to him everything that took place. I was in tears at this point and He said, "Stay where you are at, I'm on my way." I could tell that he was pissed off. Kane was there in less than 30 minutes. Kane had followed us back to Fiona's house. They were still there. Mimi and I sat in the car while Kane knocked on the door. Deon had stepped outside to speak with Kane. I don't know what he said, or how it happened. All I know is that within an hour, Pastor Kane was helping Deon load his truck, with all of his belongings. Mimi drove my car, Deon drove his truck and I drove Deon's car. We were on our way to my house. That bitch hated me. When we got to my house, our house, Pastor Kane set the both of us down. He said that he expected to see us in church on Sundays and wanted us to go through marriage counseling. I had gotten my husband back, or so I thought. I had him physically, but she owned a part of his heart. She had been there to help him deal with his pain. She had helped his bleeding wounds to heal, wounds that I caused. I didn't know what I was up against.

We were living together, but I was sick. He wasn't coming home at night. I couldn't sleep. I would call and his phone went straight to voicemail. I was catching hell and it had started to affect my work performance and appearance. I would go to work, after waiting up all night crying, with bags under my eyes. I had started losing weight from being stressed out. I was getting my payback for what I had taken him through. This situation did not feel good. I guess that's what they mean when they say,

"What goes around comes back around again." It took for Mimi to come over and cuss me out, in order for me to snap out of it.

"Bitch, what the fuck is up with you?" she asked. "I have never seen you cry over no nigga's. You are better than that. Look at you; you don't have on no clothes and your hair needs to be done. This ain't the Destiny I know" she said.

I looked at myself in the mirror and damn, she was right. I needed to eat. Mimi rolled up a blunt while I got dressed. After being out for a few hours, eating, drinking, talking and laughing I started to feel better. The next day I scheduled a hair appointment. I was about to get my life back on track. The days turned into weeks and I was still dealing with same old bullshit from Deon. Eventually, my depression turned into anger. Instead of sitting in the house crying all night, I would ride around the hood, looking for him. Where ever I saw his car parked. I would bust his windows out and flat his tires. I didn't care where it was parked at. The entire hood knew that he had a crazy wife, so they would look out for him. Whenever they saw me coming they would lie about which house he ran in. I never knew exactly where he was at. On top of all of that, Fiona was back with her children's father, and she was creeping on him with Deon. He would call me when he couldn't find her, or ask if I was with my husband. There were times when the two of us would ride around looking for them together. Ain't that some shit! On a few occasions, he had tried to holla at me, but he was not my type at all.

After going through this for months, I finally 'Let it go.' My lease was up, and I moved across town. I started seeing Stevie again. I should have followed his advice in the beginning. He listened patiently, as I got everything off my chest. "I told you to leave that nigga alone," he said.

It was as if nothing ever stopped between us, he still had my back. We were friends for life. I still am, and will always be crazy about Stevie. We had one of those relationships where, it didn't matter who the other was with we would always be down with each other.

One evening out of the blue, I receive a phone call from my estranged husband.

"Destiny, we need to talk, it's important. Can we meet somewhere?" he asked.

I agreed, but I didn't know what to expect. We met at the bar inside of Smokey Bones restaurant. This was one of our favorite spots. He said that he wanted to get back with his wife. He told me that he still loved me and that he knows he had made a mistake. Hell! We both did. He said that he wanted to honor his marriage vows to God and his wife. I still loved him and he was my husband, however I had much love for Stevie and I wasn't leaving him alone for Deon. At least not until I knew that he has left that ugly bitch alone for good.

I started going to Deon's place all the time. Sometimes to check on the kids, which were no longer little. I really just wanted to check and see if there was anybody over there. It had unofficially become my place too. I cooked, cleaned and washed clothes and then would go home. Deon started leaving the door open for me but I still didn't have a key. I didn't know that the whole time that I was riding through the hood looking for him and Fiona, that he was hitting another broad. This chick name was "Lisa." Mimi said that she was young as hell; younger than Fiona, and that she went both ways. Boy, he sure knew how to pick them. Oh my goodness! So now, there are two broads that I know about. What happened to all that crap he talked at Smokey Bones. Why didn't he have those hoes washing, cooking and cleaning? Why wasn't those hoes taking care of his children? It wasn't even about the kids they have been staying over at my place during the week and on some weekends since Deon and I first broke up. They will always be my babies, no matter how many hoes he was fucking. I will love them until the day that I die. I got a trick for Mr. Deon.

I was still taking Deon's money, and still seeing Stevie. I cut up, straight shopping, whenever I wanted, because he was still my husband. Everyone in the hood thought I was psycho. I would try to run him over with my car, if I saw him talking to a female. I had chased him and Lisa down, while I was driving his truck, on I-4. The only reason they got away is because I needed gas. He started getting creative. He would have someone to take him to drop off his car and park in crazy places around town. So if I came looking for him I wouldn't spot his car.

One evening I was at one of Stevie's spots on Ivey Lane picking up a pan of garlic crabs from a local restaurant. I was making a pitcher of apple martinis while Stevie was rolling a blunt for us to enjoy. Unbeknownst to us right outside our door was Stevie's crew deep in some shit that was causing a lot of commotion. We were chilling enjoying ourselves listening to some *Trick Daddy's Thug Holiday*. Without notice Deon came walking in the living room. He had passed by and saw my car parked outside. I don't know how the hell he got past Stevie's folks, but he did.

"What's up Destiny? Oh it's like that?" he asked.

Deon had violated all kinds of codes in my opinion. You don't just walk into nobodies shit like that I thought. Stevie stood up, "You got two fucking seconds to get the fuck out my shit, unless you wanna get carried out," he said reaching for his gun at his waist. Deon was not packing or holding nothing. I don't know where this man gets the heart from to do all that he had done. He walked out and left.

It's the weekend, and Halloween night. Mimi had V.I.P. tickets to go to a Halloween party and all of the ball players were expected to be there. This was said to be the hottest party in town. We had went to the Mall of Millennia earlier, so everything we had on was new, from head to toe. The club was packed with ballers. I mean real ballers. We had a good ass time. After the club, I decided that I wanted to see my husband. I had had one too many drinks. Mimi drove us to his apartment. It was three in the morning. I did not have a key to the gate, so we waited twenty minutes, and followed someone in.

I saw his truck parked on the side of the building, not in front of his door. "I wonder why he parked over there?" I asked Mimi. "Park right beside his truck," I told her. We walked up the stairs and knocked on the door. No answer. He had to be here, his truck was outside. "Stand Back," Mimi said, as she kicked in the door. This bitch was crazy for real. We walked all around the house, no one. The bedroom was the last room to check, and the door was closed. I opened the bedroom door, and we both walked in. Lisa and Deon are still in the bed asleep. Deon had on his boxers and she was butt naked. I didn't know which one to hit first. I had a cup of Hennessey in my hands and poured it in both of their faces. They jumped up and I swung on him first. She runs her boney ass in the bathroom and locks herself in. Mimi and I scrapped like cats and dogs. There were all kinds of noises coming from the apartment.

Mimi was yelling at me telling me it was time to leave. I didn't listen. Someone called the police and I was the only one to go to jail that night. They took me because I hadn't suffered from the attack, but Deon on the other hand was messed up. I had stabbed him multiple times with a pair of tweezers and there was blood everywhere. In the end I was the fool because he was still with Lisa and I was in jail. I was charged with domestic violence, but the charges were later dropped because Deon and Lisa wouldn't write a statement to press charges. I had to sit in jail for at least 24 hours before I was granted bond. Deon came to the police station twice to get me released and they weren't willing to grant me a bond. I never made it to the general population area of the jail. I was still in the intake area sleeping on a cold bench all night with little to no sleep. When the officer came into the holding cell to tell me I was going home, I felt like I had hit the lottery. I never knew the outdoor fresh air smelled so good. The first person I saw was Mimi and her man, Theo. He had sent his personal friend bondsman to come and get me. Mimi was my girl. She always had my back.

Mimi and I had become super tight after that. Whenever we weren't working, we were around each other all the time. Her boyfriend was crazy as hell. The two of them stayed fighting, and mostly about another female. The more they go into it, the more we hung out.

One weekend, we were getting dressed and she couldn't find her boots. She realized that she had left them over Theo's house. "We can stop to get them on our way to the club," I told her. I pulled up in the driveway and she went upstairs. "Damn Mimi, hurry up," I thought to myself. Ten minutes had passed and it seemed like forever. Five minutes later she came flying out of the house, running down the stairs. She picked up a brick from the yard and threw it in his windshield. If you knew Theo, you know that he loved his car. He drove a brand new black Cadillac Escalade truck, with chrome trimming, 24 inch spinner rims, tinted windows and suicide doors. What she do that for? He came running out the house shooting.

"Bitch get in," I screamed. This crazy man is shooting at her while she is running to my car. I punched my foot to the gas and knocked over a mailbox and trash can. "Hurry Destiny," Mimi yelled. What did she think I was trying to do? After we got a safe distance away from there I pulled over to look at my car. I had twelve bullet holes on the passenger side of my car from the front to the back. A few of the bullets had penetrated straight through to the other side of the car. What the hell were we thinking? He could have killed us. Oh Hell No! I called him snapping. "Whatever you and Mimi are going through that's between ya'll, I don't have shit to do with that. You shot at my car, you could have killed me." I yelled. I was angry, crying and still shaken. "I'm about to call the police," I said.

"No don't do that Destiny," he said. "I have to file a police report so that the insurance company can pay for the damages," I told him. He pleaded with me not to call the police. He said that he would have his folks fix the bodywork, pay for a rental car, and that he had $2000 that I could pick up now. I was cool with that. I dropped Mimi off at my house while I picked the money up. I split the money down the middle with her, and then cussed her out for getting my car shot up. Crazy hoe! After this incident, I chilled out for a while. My guardian Angel had come through again.

CHAPTER 23

It's time to go back to school and finish what I started. I was ready to advance my position, advance my income, and advance my education. I enrolled at the Junior college, for the following semester. My financial aid had been approved and I had already picked my schedule. Until classes started, I threw myself back into a lot of overtime. While I was trying to get my shit together, Mimi was out there fucking up my name. She was out and about, doing what she did best. When she would get pulled over for running a stop sign she dropped someone else's name. One night while out riding, she got caught with weed in the car, plus she had been drinking. On top of all that she has an outstanding warrant in a different county. She gave them my name. She was arrested and booked as me. Her man bonded her out before the finger prints came back. She was given a court date and never returned. A warrant was now issued in my name! I couldn't believe it; I had a warrant for my arrest. That was the falling out between me and Mimi. A real friend wouldn't do any shit like that. I understood her situation and all, but she knows too many people to be giving my name. I contacted the Orange County clerk of courts to see what my options were. I had to go downtown and get finger printed in order to verify that I actually wasn't wanted. Then I was expected to file a report for identity theft. Another warrant was issued for Me. What the hell was I suppose to do? I was working and couldn't afford to have anything like that on my record.

I had too much going for me. I was in school and working fulltime. I was still dealing with Deon and Stevie at the same damn time. Here I was still taking care of my step kids and I lost my best friend to some bullshit. I'm sick of Orlando it's time for me to go. While at work during a break I looked on the hospitals Intra-net system looking for a place that was open for a job transfer. I saw that we had a sister hospital in Atlanta. HOTLANTA! I had never been there before, but I heard that it's off the chain. Home of the finest strip clubs, Braves and the Falcons. Not to mention all of the hottest rappers are from Atlanta. I want to meet Ludacris, T.I., Lil' John, Usher, the Ying Yang Twins, JD, Young Jeezy, La'Mica, and Outkast; need I say more? It was a done deal. I had my mind set. I am moving to Atlanta.

I started calling the hospital in my department, to find out who the supervisor and the manager was. I wanted to find out if they had any positions available and who I needed to talk to. After harassing them for three weeks, I found out that someone had left on maternity leave and was not coming back. I had finally gotten an interview.

I took a two week vacation from job and drove to Atlanta for my interview. I found out through my grandmother on my dad's side that I had a cousin that lived in Decatur. She was not having me check into a hotel when she lived in a 4 bedroom house. She had two beautiful kids that were sweethearts. I came up on the weekend and my interview was on Tuesday. I enjoyed myself the whole weekend getting to know my cousins. I interviewed on Tuesday and was offered the job the same day. I found a nice one bedroom apartment right around the corner. I had paid the rent, deposit and had the utilities connected. I didn't even stay the whole two weeks.

I was back in Orlando in less than a week. I had put my two week notice in to work. I informed Stevie that I was leaving and he was very supportive. My Florida Hospital family hated to see me leave. Now, of all times Deon wants to get his shit together. He wanted his wife back. Been there and done that. How does the song go? *'I heard it all before,'* by *Sunshine Anderson* well, I had heard enough. Even though he didn't want me to leave he helped me to load the Uhaul. I was on my way to Atlanta. I had drove that huge Uhaul while pulling my car on the back all the way to ATL by myself. Once I pulled up in front of my apartment I had no idea how I was going to get all of my things out of the truck and into the house. I just knew that it had to be done. I started taking out the small things when two Mexican guys offered to help me. I gave them $20 each, ordered a pizza and bought a 12-pack of beer. Within two hours the truck was fully unloaded and my furniture was in place. It looked like I had been there for weeks.

God is so good! Monday morning I started my first day. The position that I accepted was a grade higher than the position that I'd just left. I had my own desk and my own office. My responsibilities were increased but I worked at my own pace. The hospital was a lot smaller than the one I left, and everyone knew everyone. It was like a small family. It didn't take me long before I learned how to work the highways. Where I lived was convenient to everything. The Cumberland Mall was right around the corner. I mean walking distance. Ross, TJ Maxx, Red Lobster, Apple Bee's, Olive Garden, you name it. I was also only 15 minutes from downtown Atlanta. I worked Monday through Friday, no weekends. I went to the gym in my apartment complex twice during the week after work. Two days out of the week I would go to Barnes and Nobles after work. Of course, I found out where the parties and clubs were. All you had to do was listen to the radio. I didn't mind hanging out by myself. Sometimes that's when you had the most fun. The local sports bars had become my thing. Certain nights would be open mic and others nights would be karaoke. Certain nights would be comedy night and certain nights were bingo. Atlanta was full of sports bars. I began to mingle and meet people.

What I did notice about most people that I met, everyone had a hustle. No matter what your 9 to 5 consisted of, there was always a hustle after work. The restaurants and sports bars were packed during happy hour after work. People gathered together and socialized while waiting for the traffic to die down. This is where I met a lot of professional working class people. During these hours a lot of networking took place. People passed around business cards to everyone trying to get their hustle on. I had never seen so many black people doing so well. Everyone was driving nice brand new cars and lived in well to do neighborhoods. I was tired of my Mercedes and tired of seeing the same old rims. I wanted a new ride something a little classier. I needed a hustle something I was good at and something that came natural.

I was at the flea market in West End with one of my coworkers. We walked around just browsing and checking out prices of things. I couldn't believe how cheap some of the name brand clothing was. It wasn't all authentic but it still was a good deal. I started up a conversation with one of the African store owners. He wouldn't tell me what he was paying for the items however we worked out a deal. If I spent an amount at least $500 and purchased items in bulk then he would give me wholesale prices. I had my hustle. Every other week I would need new items. I started selling clothes and purses out the trunk of my car. I didn't care where I was at I was selling my stuff. It got to the point where my phone was constantly ringing. I ordered business cards online and called my business, 'Clothes on the Go'. I was more than doubling my money. Each time I re-up, I spent more money. Business was good. I had even ran up on the contact number of the person he shopped with. It was really on now. I had cut out the middle man. Money started flowing in by the boat load. It was time to hit up Club Visions and celebrate my new pay grade.

CHAPTER 24: THE ECLIPSE

After the car flipped two to three times on the highway, a Good Samaritan pulled over and ran to the car. It was upside down, and I was in and out of consciousness. I finally realize what God has been trying to tell me all along. Father I understand now. I finally understand what my mother was trying to teach me. All this time, I had been searching for the love of a mother and father. But what I failed to realize, is that everything I had been searching for, I already possessed. God loves me, and has always had my back. It was myself that I had been running from. I'm tired of running, it's time to stop.

Lord, I'm not ready to go yet. What about my sister, and my niece? They need me. Where are you Momma? I am being pulled out of the car, to the side of the road. The air smells of gasoline. I can't breathe. I am carried away by a set of strong arms through the fire and flames. My car is on fire. My eyes are heavy. I can't keep them open.

I was slowly awakened from a deep sleep with many questions. Where am I? Was I in an accident? Still dazed and confused I tried to open my eyes to focus and I started noticing my surroundings. My clothes were gone, replaced by a hospital gown. How long had I been here? One of my arms was handcuffed to the side of the bed.

There was a police officer standing in the back of the room, near the doorway. There was also someone standing beside my bed. It was the person who had pulled me from the car. Hold on, I've seen him somewhere before. This can't be who I think it is. Was I dreaming? I blinked my eyes twice and he was still standing there. It was "Drake" my king. He was in the flow of traffic and saw the entire accident take place. He hadn't left my side since he pulled me from the car.

ABOUT THE AUTHOR

Lakeesha was born in Mississippi to a single mother. She had the privilege of living in many different states including Florida, Alabama, and Georgia during her lifetime. She went to college in Florida where she still resides and manage a region of a multi-million dollar corporation. She has been writing poems and short stories for twenty years and was recently encouraged to try her hand at writing her first novel. It didn't take long for her to come up with her exciting debut novel, Little Lost Girl: Journey of a Soldier. Be on the look out for a sequel to this critically acclaimed novel inspired by the author's real life experiences.

Made in the USA
Columbia, SC
22 July 2017